BACK

BACK TO BAYOU SABINE

A Bayou Sabine Novella

LAUREN FAULKENBERRY

Blue Crow Books

Publisher's Cataloging-in-Publication Data
Faulkenberry, Lauren 1978-.
Back to Bayou Sabine : A Bayou Sabine Novella / Lauren Faulkenberry.
p._____ cm._____
ISBN 978-1-947834-17-0 (Pbk) | ISBN 978-1-947834-18-7 (eBook)
1. Women—Louisiana—Fiction. 2. Love—Fiction. 3. Louisiana—Fiction. I. Title.
813'.6—dc23 | 2017955912

Blue Crow Books

Published by Blue Crow Books
an imprint of Blue Crow Publishing, LLC, Chapel Hill, NC
www.bluecrowpublishing.com
Cover Photograph by TK
Cover Design by Lauren Faulkenberry

First published by Velvet Morning Press as
First Blue Crow Books Edition 2017

Praise for The Bayou Sabine Series

Beautifully descriptive and engaging. A delightful story about learning to let go of who you think you need to be and take a risk on happiness.

—Orly Konig, author of THE DISTANCE HOME and founding president of the Women's Fiction Writers Association.

Faulkenberry is a gifted storyteller with the ability to capture the most human side of relationships. *Bayou Whispers* is a rich and emotional story that will draw readers into the heat of the bayou and leave them wanting more.

–Tina Ann Forkner, award-winning author of THE REAL THING and WAKING UP JOY

I'd read this book again, and I recommend it to others who love a fast-paced romantic mystery. I give this book five stars.

- Dayna Leigh Cheser, author of the TIME series

I loved this book. It has so many different dimensions that you will literally be glued to the pages...There's mystery, intrigue, and unexpected pieces to the story. PICK UP THIS BOOK. It's a MUST READ.

- Pretty Little Book Reviews

From the moment Jack spoke in that French/Creole drawl he and Faulkenberry had me hook, line and sinker. I was a goner, and I didn't surface until the novel's end. I may be in love.

- Page One Books

Faulkenberry creates a world of magic, suspense, and desire. An engrossing romance with just the right amount of heat!

- Julie C. Gardner, author of LETTERS FOR SCARLET

Also by Lauren Faulkenberry

BAYOU MY LOVE: A Bayou Sabine Novel

BACK TO BAYOU SABINE: A Bayou Sabine Novella

BAYOU WHISPERS: A Bayou Sabine Novel

JUST THE TROUBLE I NEEDED: A Bayou Sabine Novella

BENEATH OUR SKIN and Other Stories

sign up for Lauren's author newsletter,

Writing Down South:

tinyletter.com/firebrandpress

for Aunt Molly

Chapter One
_____

THE HOUSE on Buchanan Street was just as awful as I feared it
would be. The whole street was filled with two-story painted
brick houses that were no doubt something to behold back in
their heyday (circa 1910 based on the columns and balconies
out front). Now, because they were so close to the university, too
many of them had been rented out to students. The grass was
dappled with beer cans. Windows that had likely seen the last
days of Prohibition were now obstructed by hand-painted
banners with Greek letters. In general, I tried not to drive down
these streets because it was so infuriating to imagine what the
insides of these houses looked like.

I knew what they should have inside: carved crown
molding, clawfoot tubs and art-deco tile. Long cherry tables that
sat eight to ten dinner guests and mahogany chairs with ball-
and-claw feet.

What they actually held were overstuffed couches that had
been plucked from the curbs. Dining rooms and sitting rooms
had been split apart to make more bedrooms, the sheetrock

thrown up so hastily that the nails were popping out. Original hardwood floors had been overlaid with vinyl flooring that was easy to clean and then tear out later.

I parked on the opposite side of the street and reached for my coffee. Mike sat next to me, sending one more text message while holding a doughnut in his teeth. He was thirty-five but didn't look it. He'd been working for my father for five years and had quickly earned his respect—a feat I had never been able to accomplish in all of my thirty-one years. I'd spent the last ten working for my father in his house-flipping business, but I was the only one on the team who hadn't been allowed to take the lead on a project.

"You think they've got the grossest parts done with?" I asked.

Mike grinned, and a blob of crème filling dropped from the doughnut onto his shirt. "Enza, you're a far cry from a girlie girl but saying things like 'grossest' gets you awfully damn close."

"My father knows I hate cleaning up after frat boys more than anything else in this world."

Mike wiped the cream from his shirt and licked his finger. "Still mad at you, is he?"

I took a sip of coffee and cringed as a pile of debris sailed out of the upstairs window and into the trash bin below. There was a crash, then a puff of dust that rose like a cloud.

"We should have hazmat suits," I said.

"It won't be that bad."

I snorted. "Don't you remember what your college apartment was like at the end of the semester?"

He popped the last bit of doughnut into his mouth and sighed. "Why'd you have to go and ruin a perfectly average morning? Don't you know that sometimes you just need to go in with zero expectations?"

There was another crash as chunks of linoleum fell from the window.

"Let's get this over with," I said.

THE HOUSE we were flipping was on the corner, on the fringe of the fraternity houses. It had been rented to students as well, but mercifully it hadn't been split into apartments. It was a hearty Italianate style, with a couple of bedrooms upstairs, a sunroom full of windows off the kitchen, and hand-carved decorative trim on the outside eaves. If I could have picked it up and moved it about eight blocks away, I'd have lived in it myself.

The house had gone into foreclosure, so my father had bought it for nearly nothing. He was flipping it (or more accurately, his crew was flipping it) with the hopes of selling it as a single-family home. One thing I admired about my father was his tenacity. He hated to see these houses decline as much as I did, and he took every opportunity to salvage them from landlords who ushered them into disrepair.

But here's the thing about a foreclosure: People leave the house all hacked off, which means it's the worst kind of wreck when we get inside. They leave behind dirty clothes, garbage, litter boxes, a refrigerator full of rotting food. When the inhabitants are students leaving at the end of the semester, then the landlord has exactly zero cares about what's left behind—in fact, it seems the landlord instructs those tenants to leave everything, just as an additional salute to the bank. Unfortunately, that doesn't affect the bank. A house sold "as-is" means that the lucky buyer inherits all of its filth. That's the price you pay for getting a house ultra-cheap. You have to be willing to deal with all of the grossness in the beginning in order to reap the benefits in the end. And in the end, I'm usually happy with our results. Dad's team takes these houses that might as well have "do not resuscitate" stamped on their doors and transforms them into homes again. The feeling of triumph that comes when I walk through a house we've finished almost makes up for all the hassle I have with my father.

Almost.

INSIDE, Dad's first-string crew was working on the upstairs, tearing out carpet from the bedrooms. They sent Mike and me downstairs to rip up the linoleum in the kitchen. It was only spring, but it felt like summer. Even with the air conditioner on, we sweat through our clothes in minutes.

Most of the linoleum was a beige pattern that looked like woven straw, but some sections had a geometric pattern done in gold and olive green, apparently left exposed by the removal of an appliance or an island. As we shoved the stove into the hallway, we unearthed a section of bright orange and brown.

"Look," Mike said, "it's like a time capsule for floor covering. Hello, 1975."

"Guess it was too much trouble to move these the first time around," I said. I was hardly surprised by people's laziness any more.

Mike tossed me a crowbar, and we started at opposite corners of the kitchen, prying up the scarred linoleum. This was day three of demo, so I was spared the most gruesome of the frat-boy fallout. Mike had been on this project from the start, but my father had switched me over to this house after I'd made the executive decision to enhance the curb appeal at his last flip, across the way in a historic part of Durham, North Carolina. I'd spent eight hundred dollars on landscaping, which included sod, some hedges and a crepe myrtle tree to add a splash of color to a grim little lot that had about three feet of yard all the way around it. The house was cute enough—a small two-story with a new porch—but it needed some plants in the yard as proof that life forms could actually survive there. My father had stopped me when I had a landscaper plot out a small flower bed by the porch and bring a truckload of wood chips. I had two pallets of daylilies and hostas in the back of my company pickup truck, which he'd insisted I return for a full refund.

"That was money wasted," my father had barked, glaring at my grass-stained jeans. "And you set us back three days."

"Nobody wants a house that looks barren," I said.

He cursed all the way back to his truck and slammed the door.

That was two days ago. The pickup was now parked in my backyard, lilies and hostas intact. I had no intention of returning them.

This morning, my dad had sent Mike to pick me up, presumably so I couldn't rebel and drive over to the Durham house to unleash more unwanted beautification. Mike had faithfully driven me over here, explaining that this one needed my help more.

But I knew better. Mike was a bad liar.

"He'll get over it," Mike said, tossing a scrap of lino onto the pile in the corner. "You'll be out of the penalty box soon enough."

I laughed. "Please. Dad never gets over anything."

Even with his dust mask on, I could tell he was grinning from the little wrinkles at the corners of his eyes.

"That house needed landscaping," he said. "It'll sell faster for it, but you knew that."

I shrugged, sliding the crowbar under the vinyl to pop the next section up. "He'll never admit I was right."

"He'll see it, though."

"But now it's only half-landscaped," I said, "which makes us look lazy."

Mike was no doubt the son my father always wished he'd had. A few years older than me, he had a wife who was mild-mannered and not what my father would call "willful." He had twin two-year-old sons and lived in an old historic house he'd rescued from foreclosure and renovated himself. He was reliable like Toyota sedans. They'll always get you where you want to go and rarely give you any hassle. My father set Mike on all the best houses—the ones that had real character and style that could showcase Mike's carpentry skills. And he had real skills, that man. I'd seen him replicate hand-carved crown molding and Victorian newel posts in some of the most expensive houses Dad had invested in. They'd once invited members of the Historical Society to a special open house reception and even the president couldn't tell which parts of the woodwork Mike had rebuilt.

I, however, felt like a sand spur in my father's shoe. He called me "willful" in that way that means "pain in the ass." He had permanent frown lines from our arguments over the years, and he challenged every suggestion I put forth. Mike could have his run of any project, but Dad second-guessed every decision I made. He frequently went behind my back to change plans I'd made with contractors. I was always hopeful that my current project would be the one to change his mind about me, and that the next one would be the one where he set me loose.

I'd once confessed this to Kate, my best friend. She'd scoffed and said, "Enza, that is the very definition of insanity. Doing the same thing over and over, and each time expecting different results."

"But each house has different variables," I argued. "That means the potential for different outcomes."

"Not when your father is the constant."

Kate and I had gone to college together. She'd studied biology and had a clear understanding of the scientific method. She'd been rewarded with a job in one of the many research firms in the Triangle area. I'd majored in English and fumbled my way through lots of dead-end jobs before finally working for my father full time. If anyone could recognize a pattern, it was Kate.

We complemented each other well. She was a little over five feet tall with shoulder-length blond hair that she kept perfectly straight and smooth. I towered over her and could barely fit my forearm in her skinny jeans. My hair was curly and dark, and refused to stay tamed when the humidity was above forty percent. In general, Kate looked librarian-chic, and I looked like I'd just rolled out of bed. Kate preferred pencil skirts, and I was happy in jeans, but when it came to the things that mattered, we were as well-matched as two friends could be. I wouldn't have survived working for my father so long if it hadn't been for her.

"Hey," Mike said. "You want to do the honors?" He held the sledgehammer out to me, and a smile touched the corner of his mouth.

The nasty Formica countertops had to go too. Mike knew I had a secret love for the sledgehammer.

"You sure?" I asked, running my fingers along the counter. It had scratches and cigarette burns, deep gouges from someone using it as a cutting board.

"I like to watch," he said, and winked.

I tried not to think of my father as I swung. I didn't want to use so much force I'd damage the cabinets below. Mike pulled his safety glasses on, and I swung, feeling the shock wave ripple along my arms and down my back. There was nothing quite as satisfying as that tingling sensation of momentum meeting resistance.

"Ah," he said, holding his hand against his chest. "I do love the sound of a large hammer making contact."

"That's the sound of getting shit done," I said, and swung again.

It was after lunch when my father dropped by to check up on us. By then we had all of the original floors exposed. The kitchen had broad pine boards that could be refinished. In the bathrooms, the original tile was gone, but I envisioned installing a checkered pattern that would give a nod to the 1920s.

Mike and I were in the bathroom, tearing out the busted sink when the *clack-clack* of my father's expensive loafers echoed down the hall.

"Looks like you're making good progress here," he said to Mike.

"Oh, you know how we love ripping things apart," Mike said.

"Not afraid of the dirty work," my father said, shifting his gaze toward me.

I'd added it up in my head one day: Since college, I'd worked on nearly fifty houses with my father's crew. I'd painted, sanded and caulked my way into this business, and earned enough respect from the guys that they didn't resent me for being the boss's daughter. But I was the only one who had to get his approval for every decision I made.

"Enza," he said at last, "I need to talk to you for a minute."

Mike shot me a sympathetic look as I followed my father out onto the porch.

"News on the Durham house?" I couldn't wait for him to have to tell me it had sold.

He leaned against the porch railing and crossed his arms over his chest. "This is something else."

His furrowed brow made me uneasy.

"It's Vergie," he said. "She passed away."

He said it matter-of-factly, like he was giving me a budget for cabinetry.

The air rushed out of my lungs as I sat down on the rail next to him. "How?" I finally said.

He shrugged. "Heart attack, I think. I thought you might want to know."

I stared at him, surprised that even he would say it with such a lack of emotion.

"When?" I asked.

"Yesterday. I guess we were still on a list of contacts somewhere."

I stared at the floorboards of the porch. The white paint was peeling off, revealing light blue underneath. My father sighed as if he had other things he'd rather be doing. My grandmother Vergie likely hadn't crossed his mind in a decade.

"When's the funeral?"

He glanced at his watch. "Friday."

"Are you going?"

He raised an eyebrow and stood. "No."

"Well, I guess I'm going to have to ask for a few days off."

My father glared at me with a mix of pity and frustration. The hard muscle of his jaw twitched.

"Don't give me that look, Dad. I know you're still mad about the landscaping, but we both know you don't need me for this demo. The guys can handle it just fine."

He shook his head and muttered, "After what she did to us, I can't see why you want anything to do with that family."

"Vergie wasn't Mom," I said.

He sighed and walked back toward his car.

"It's only a couple of days," I said. "I'll be back and can help with the rest of the repairs."

"We'll see about that." He climbed into the car and backed out of the driveway without giving me another glance.

I SHOULDN'T HAVE BEEN SURPRISED. Vergie was my grandmother, but I hadn't seen her in fifteen years. She was my mom's mother, and my mom had left my dad and me back when I was sixteen. Dad refused to talk about my mother, and he would never offer me details about what had happened. He made it sound like my mother just up and left with no explanation. For the longest time, I assumed that was true. After my mom was gone, he cut Vergie out of our lives too. She lived down in a little town called Bayou Sabine, not too far from New Orleans. When I was a kid, I'd spent my summers with her. My mother wanted me to experience the kind of life she had growing up. We were doing well in North Carolina, but she missed Louisiana and told me once that she felt like her new home was too fast-paced. She wanted me to see what it was like to live in a quiet rural place too.

Vergie had been one of my favorite people, but after my mother left, Dad put a stop to the visits. He'd caught me trying to take a bus to Bayou Sabine that first summer without Mom, so he grounded me for two months. We'd screamed at each other until he'd finally said, "Your mother doesn't want anything else to do with us, and neither does Vergie."

His words had hit me like stones. I'd never thought Vergie wouldn't want to see me again either. The idea of showing up at her door only to have her slam it in my face filled me with humiliation.

After that, I didn't make any more attempts to visit my grandmother. Years later, I began to wonder if my father had been truthful, but I was too afraid to find out. What if I went to see her and she sent me away just like I'd imagined? I didn't have any reason to think he'd lied.

But the way he acted a few minutes ago as he talked about Vergie made me think he was hiding something. And had been for a long time.

Chapter Two

KATE MET me at our favorite dive bar at nine. She was the exact opposite of me in a lot of ways but most obviously in her appreciation of fashion. Today she wore a short dress with a bright blue pattern that made her eyes look turquoise. Her hair was pulled back into a ponytail that played up the angles in her cheekbones. Kate had legs like a ballerina and had likely never been lonely in her whole life. A man in a tan suit held the door for her as she entered and waved to me.

"Hey, Enza," she said, sliding into the booth. "What's wrong? You look like something the cat threw up."

Kate never had time for delicacy.

I took a sip of my bourbon as she flagged down the waiter and ordered a martini.

"And why are you wearing that?" she asked. "I told you to wear something cute."

I glanced down at my blouse—only a little wrinkled—and my jeans with a hole in the thigh.

"I changed from my work clothes," I said. "It could have been worse."

She frowned.

"What? I'm wearing heels."

"Beat-up cowboy boots don't count as 'heels.'" She reached over and fluffed my hair.

"What is wrong with you?" I said, pulling away.

"Ah. You forgot."

"Forgot what?"

"I told a friend of mine to meet us here," she said.

"Oh come on, Kate. I've had the worst day. I don't feel like being set up tonight."

"Too bad," she said. "He's already on his way." The waiter set a martini in front of her and smiled. "Thanks," she said to him. Turning to me, she said, "You'll like him. He's funny."

I shook my head. "Can you call him and tell him I got sick or something?"

"Nope."

"Kate, I can't do this tonight."

"Yes you can. You need to get back on the horse. With a man who has a job and pays his own rent. You're not allowed to date fixer-uppers any more."

I didn't have a great track record with dating. My taste in men was too often like my taste in houses: They were well-designed, but had serious structural damage that required too much maintenance and repair.

Kate, however, overcompensated by finding the most boring men in the Triangle area. The last man she'd forced me to have dinner with was a tax accountant who didn't move his lips when he kissed me.

"My grandmother died," I said. "Cut me a break."

She stared at me for a minute, as if deciding whether I was joking. At last she said, "Shit, Enza. I'm sorry."

I took another sip of bourbon. "I hadn't seen her in fifteen years. Not since Mom left us."

"Oh," she said, twirling the martini glass.

"We were close when I was little. I used to spend every summer with her."

"God," she said, her eyebrows scrunching together. "I'm really sorry."

"The funeral's Friday," I said. "Down in Louisiana. I thought I'd go."

"You want some company?"

"You want to be my date to a funeral?"

She shrugged. "It sucks going to those things alone. We could both stand to get out of here for a couple of days. You can take that time to explain what's wrong with the men I set you up with so I can be more efficient with my hunting."

"Right," I said.

She sipped her drink. "Come on, these things don't have to be miserable."

"I think that's the tagline of the local funeral home."

She shrugged. "I'm coming with you. It's settled. You're too tired to make smart decisions. I can tell."

"Fine," I said, rolling my eyes. I hated the idea of being a stranger there, knowing no one. Why had I not tried to get in touch with Vergie for all those years? Why had I let my father make me think she didn't care about me any more? She couldn't possibly have felt that way, could she?

"Hey," Kate said. "Why don't we stay a couple extra days and just relax? Take a girls' trip like we used to?"

"A funeral is a terrible excuse for a vacation."

"It's not a vacation," she said. "It's a mandatory decompression session. You've been working way too hard and way too much. When's the last time you took time off?"

I frowned, counting back one month at a time.

"Exactly," she said. "Let's just stay a couple extra days and get you back on the spectrum of normal."

"I don't feel right doing that."

"Make it a tribute to your grandmother," she said. "Let's go to some of her favorite places."

"My dad will have a fit if I take so much time off work."

"So let him!" She gestured with her martini, sloshing some onto the table. "Your dad is what you become when you never take a vacation. Do you really want to be him in twenty years?"

My eye twitched at the thought.

"Oh, hey," she said. "There's David."

Before I could bolt, David was standing by the table and reaching for my hand. He wore a salmon-colored shirt with a hideous striped tie, and he shook my hand way too hard. His blond hair was cropped short, and his khakis were much too baggy for his lean frame.

"What's up?" David said. He pulled up a chair, and I shot Kate my most baleful look.

She glanced at her phone and said, "Oh my gosh, I have to take this call. I'm so sorry."

I glared at her, but she only winked at me and strode up to the bar, where I knew she would order another drink and chat with the bartender. After thirty minutes, she'd check up on us, and when I gave her my S.O.S. look, she'd tell me she wasn't feeling well, and I'd insist on taking her home, despite her protests.

I humored her, meeting these men she found, because she genuinely thought I'd like them. And I usually did like them— just not enough to see them again. For all of her time spent predicting patterns in microorganisms, she had zero ability to predict human chemistry.

Chapter Three

WE FLEW into New Orleans and rented a compact car with a hatchback. It looked like a June bug, but it was zippy and easy to park—a fact we both appreciated after taking a full five minutes to find a place to parallel park by the first coffee shop we saw. Kate sat in the passenger seat with a notebook and a road atlas, her bare feet propped on the dash. I didn't mind driving, and we were safer that way. Kate drove like she was on a race track and yelled at other drivers who shared her bad behavior. The last time I let her drive, she nearly ran over a pedestrian while passing a dump truck and flipping off the driver. Kate weighed about a hundred pounds soaking wet, but she wasn't intimidated by anything. Especially when driving.

"Don't you want to go to her house?" Kate asked. She scanned the list I'd made in my notebook of possible places to visit. I'd spent the whole flight thinking about places Vergie and I had gone together when I was a kid, but they all seemed too touristy now. We'd had coffee every Sunday at the Café du

Monde; we'd done tours at the famous cemeteries, ridden the trolley, gone to the jazz museum. We'd wandered through Jackson Square and the riverside market, and done all of the things people do when they visit the city. I'd written all those places down but going to them now didn't feel like anything special.

"No," I said. "I don't."

She turned and stared at me. "Why not?"

I took the next exit off the Interstate, onto a two-lane highway north of the city. "There'll be tons of people there, for the wake."

"So?"

"So, I can't handle seeing all those people who knew her so well. I don't want to have to explain who I am and what happened."

"Just say you're a friend, and leave it at that. You don't have to explain anything."

"When has anybody in the South ever settled for a short answer like that?"

"We can be the mysterious strangers. They'll leave us alone."

I laughed. "Not even."

She shrugged. "Your call."

The highway carried us parallel to a canal where egrets dotted the trees. The tops of the cypresses were bright green but looked almost black in the shadows. I rolled the window down just enough to smell the salty air. Kate searched the radio stations until she found classic rock, then turned it up and started singing along, badly, to *Whole Lotta Love*.

After a while, we came to a state park that was situated on a bend in the river. As soon as I saw the historic two-story white house, I knew it was the right place.

"What's this?" Kate asked.

"Vergie used to bring me here. There's a beach."

"It looks like alligator heaven."

"Probably."

We got out of the car and walked past the house, onto a trail that led to the beach. The buzzing of katydids made my skin tingle as we walked through the cypress grove, curtains of moss hanging from the massive limbs of the trees. We wound through the grove until we came to a clearing where half a dozen people were scattered on the shore. The bright blue of the lake made the sand look white. I pulled off my boots and socks, and walked toward the water.

"Hey," Kate called out, "wait up."

I stopped at the shore and let the waves wash over my feet. As I stared out into the blue-green of the lake, I was struck by an image of Vergie and me in a canoe. I'd borrowed one of her big floppy sun hats, and she was teaching me to paddle. I was about twelve. She'd handed me an oar and said, "If you ever go out in a boat with a boy, you make sure you know how to swim and paddle. They'll try hard to impress you, but you better know how to row yourself out of there."

Vergie had been alone as far back as I could remember. My grandfather died a few years after he and Vergie had married, and I'd never known her to have another man in her life. I hadn't thought much about that when I was a girl, but now I wondered why she'd made that choice. I knew it was she who'd made a choice, because Vergie was beautiful and smart and fearless. She'd no doubt been pursued by half the men in the parish. I remembered men bringing her gifts, doing work around the house as favors. When I was young, I just thought they were being neighborly, but thinking about it now, I realized they were all likely chasing after her. Had she chosen to stay single because she couldn't love anyone the way she'd loved my grandfather? Could she just not imagine herself with anyone else? I didn't think of Vergie as being that much of a romantic, but maybe she was.

If it hadn't been for my father, I never would have imagined her not wanting to see me any more, either.

And now, the more I thought about the situation, the more I was beginning to doubt my father. It had been easy for my sixteen-year-old brain to assume Vergie didn't want to see me because of what had happened with my parents. I was sure she hated my father, and by extension, I figured she hated me. I thought back to the moment he said I would no longer be visiting Vergie. *She doesn't want you to visit any more,* he'd said. Could I really picture my grandmother saying such a thing? No. I'd been a fool.

KATE TROTTED over to me and pulled her hair back into a ponytail. It looked nearly platinum in the sunlight.

"How about we stay here a while?" I suggested.

She stared out over the water, then at me.

"You OK?" she asked.

"I just want to spend the day somewhere quiet. No tourists."

Kate smiled and then sat down on the sand. "Let's see if we can get some tan lines, then," she said, and hitched her skirt up high on her thighs.

Chapter Four

WE'D BOOKED a room in a bed and breakfast in Algiers, just across the lake from New Orleans. Vergie's funeral was being held in a little church in Bayou Sabine, but there were no places to stay there. Bayou Sabine was really more of a community than a town; it had a fire department, a post office and a couple of restaurants. With three stoplights and one gas station, it was a far cry from what I was accustomed to in Raleigh. But it had charm that sucked you in and made you want to stay a while. People did everything more slowly down here, and at this particular moment, that was exactly what I wanted. My life was generally crammed with deadlines. Every day was a constant rearranging of orders and repairs, and every person I dealt with wanted his or her problem solved yesterday.

On the porch of the Dauphine Inn, Kate and I sat at a table for two, halfway through a bottle of wine.

"I'm glad you invited yourself along on this trip," I said.

She clinked her glass against mine. "You're welcome."

"I wouldn't want to be there alone tomorrow."

She nodded slowly. "I know."

All around us, the night birds were beginning to call to each other in the trees. The inn had tiny lights strung across the porch beams and in the branches of the oak tree in the yard. A moth fluttered against the string above us.

"I think I'm going to quit my job," I said.

"What?"

"He's driving me crazy. I've been there ten years, and he still treats me like I'm a teenager."

"But you love doing houses," she said as she topped off our glasses.

"I'd love it better if I was working for myself."

"Can you do that right now?"

I had burned through most of my savings when I bought my own house. My father paid me well, which was the one reason it was so hard to leave. I'd been considering it for a while, but I had no real financial cushion to last me while my business hatched.

"No. That's the kicker. I'm stuck with him, unless I want to go work for someone else."

"That's a serious bridge to burn," she said.

I nodded. "I'm tempted to leave him and work for another company while I save some money, but I'd never hear the end of it. He obviously considers me weak and barely trustworthy. Quitting would just make him think all his doubting was justified, and then he'd be really insufferable."

She frowned as I sipped my wine.

"Damn," she said.

"Stupidly poetic, isn't it?" I said. "How the biggest fixer-upper around here is me."

Kate smirked. "Oh, please. You're no fixer-upper. You're just going through a rough patch. We all have them, and in the end we're better because of them."

I clinked my glass against hers. "You, Kate, are my favorite person in the whole world."

"I know," she said with a shrug.

THE FUNERAL WAS at ten in the morning, before the day turned to sweltering. With a breeze it was bearable, but my clothes were sticking to me anyway. North Carolina had hot summers, but Louisiana was a special brand of sultry. Since we'd arrived, I'd felt like I was on the inside of a wood stove. Heavy with humidity, the air seemed thick and hard to breathe. The best part of the day was taking a cold shower at the inn.

The church in Bayou Sabine was on the historical register as one of the oldest ones left in the parish. The white one-room building had burned four times, once during the Civil War. It had carved wooden doors with small round stained glass windows that looked almost like the portholes of a ship. When the bells rang, a flock of pigeons burst from the steeple.

I slipped my sunglasses back on and hoped no one would recognize me. It had been fifteen years, but old southerners had the uncanny ability to pick you out of a lineup long after you'd seen them last. For the first time in my adult life, I was wearing a wide-brimmed hat, a black one I'd borrowed from Kate. With her hair pulled back and her huge sunglasses on, she looked like Jackie Kennedy. I imagined I looked more like one of the British royals, mocked in the tabloids for fashion faux pas.

At the door, a gray-haired man in a suit handed us a folded paper with Vergie's picture on it. I held it tight as we stepped inside. The chapel was full. With only a dozen small pews, it would comfortably seat around seventy people. Some folding chairs had been set up as extra seating, and people were standing all along the aisles, fanning themselves with their booklets.

Kate and I stepped just inside the doorway and stood against the wall. After getting several disapproving looks, we both removed our glasses, and I tugged the brim of my hat down over my eyes.

Two gray-haired ladies walked in behind us and shuffled up one of the rows. A young man stood as they passed him, then took one of them by the elbow to steer them toward the pew where he'd been sitting. They beamed at him as they eased into the pew, and the man walked to the back corner near us.

He was tall, over six feet, with dark hair that came just past his ears. He wore a pale gray suit that was tight across his broad shoulders. He looked at us, and I quickly glanced away. Kate nudged me with her elbow, and when I looked at her, she had a hint of a smile, her eyes fixed on him.

"Maybe we need to expand your search into a different state," she whispered.

"Stop."

"He looks compassionate, financially stable and not entirely vanilla."

"You got that from one gesture?"

She spoke close to my ear as the organist began to play. "Extrapolating data. It's what I do best."

"Researching for the big guns has given you a big head."

She shrugged. "I stand by my findings."

I glanced back at the dark-haired man. He had a hint of stubble on his cheek, and I sighed, thinking of the last time I'd felt that pleasant scratch against my shoulder, my neck. He turned toward me, and I was struck by the deep blue of his eyes. I quickly looked away, dropping the pamphlet on the floor. When I picked it up, Kate whispered, "Sweet Jesus, they didn't make men like that where I grew up."

"Shhh," I whispered.

"I'm just saying, he's no fixer-upper."

Staring at Vergie's picture brought me back to the present. Her warm smile made me think again of how foolish I'd been to believe she didn't want me around. I felt tears forming as the writing on the page began to blur. Everyone stood to sing a hymn. I glanced at Kate and started mouthing the words, though I hadn't sung in a church since I was three feet tall. I was glad we were stuffed in the back so we could slip out as soon as it was over and dodge all the chatter that was bound to follow. Two days ago, I figured I'd come down here, pay my respects and close off this part of my history. But so far, being back in Bayou Sabine was just making all of my fragmented memories more vivid. It was awakening a part of me I'd forgotten, a part I hadn't known I wanted to remember.

Three more women squeezed in next to us, and my chest tightened. We stepped closer to the corner to give the ladies some room, and Kate whispered, "Are you OK?"

The room began to blur.

"Yeah," I breathed.

"Liar. What's the matter?"

I glanced around the chapel, letting my eyes rest briefly on every woman wearing black. Most of the people there were older, close to Vergie's age.

"What if my mother's here?"

"What?" she said, so loudly that a few heads turned.

I bowed my head and whispered in her ear. "My mother could be here."

Her mouth dropped open. "I thought your mother was dead."

"I never said that."

"Enza, you certainly did!"

"I said she was as good as dead," I whispered. A woman stepped up to the pulpit and started to sing a cappella, a hymn I didn't recognize.

"I can't believe you," Kate said.

"Well, to me she *was* dead. I never expected to see her again and certainly hadn't planned on it happening here."

"Shit," she muttered, and put her sunglasses back on.

WHEN MY MOTHER LEFT, I'd pestered my father for explanations, but the only thing he would say was, "She no longer wants to be with us." Now and again, I'd heard them fighting but hadn't thought anything of it. After all, my friends said their parents yelled at each other and slammed doors. It seemed my parents were just like everybody else's.

Everything had happened quite simply. My mother was there one day when I went to school, and then when I came home, she was gone. She'd left no phone number, no address, and Dad said the best thing I could do was pretend she'd never been in our lives at all.

Over the years, I'd made up all kinds of scenarios to fill in the blanks. Sometimes I imagined her running away with another man. Then later, after college enlightened me, another woman. Why else would she leave so suddenly? What else would shut my father down so completely?

Sometimes I'd picture her flying to the West Coast, or driving to Canada to start her life over in a completely different climate. When I was younger, I pictured her working in a diner or a café, maybe even in Europe, because didn't runaway mothers want to get as far away as possible from their homes?

When I got older, I wondered if it was something sinister my father had done. There were days when I fantasized about seeing her again, trying to imagine what I could say to her, what she would say to me.

Sometimes I imagined she'd left us because she had a terminal disease and wanted to spare us the hurt of watching her die. That made it easier for me to understand why she had never, ever tried to get in touch with me as years went on.

In my mind, she had left everyone she knew, including Vergie. After all, if she could cut ties with her own daughter, she could easily cut them with her mother too. But now, standing in the back of this stuffy little church, sweat running down the backs of my thighs, I realized I could have been dead wrong about all of it. My mother could have moved back to her native Louisiana.

She could be right here in this room.

It was the simplest answer of all, and I'd never allowed myself to think it might be true.

It was the most crushing answer of all.

There was a shuffling as everyone stood and opened their hymnals again. The organist started up, and the air vibrated as they launched into *I'll Fly Away*. My heart hammered against my ribs, and I fanned myself with the booklet. The voices around us grew louder until they filled the church and spilled out the windows, and a flash of memory hit me like a punch— Vergie pulling weeds in her garden, her big floppy hat hanging over her eyes as she sang the same verse—*Hallelujah by and by, I'll fly away*. I felt a catch in my chest as the tears came, and then the room closed around me so tight it felt like my ribs would crack.

I pushed past Kate and muttered an apology as I squeezed by a man near the open door.

Outside wasn't much better, but there was a hint of a breeze. The sky had darkened as rain began to drizzle, but the katydids droned on. I strode out into the grass.

"Enza," Kate said, rushing to me. "Are you OK?"

My chest heaved with each breath, but still the yard spun around me.

"I just needed a minute," I said.

She nodded, rubbing my back like I'd been choking.

"Did you see her?" Kate asked, looking back in the church. "Is she here?"

"No. It was just so hot in there. I felt like I was going to faint."

She steered me over to the front steps, and we sat. The music from inside seemed to fill the whole sky. For a long time, we said nothing as I tamped down the memories of my mother and Vergie that had begun overlapping like double-exposed photographs. Was my mother still alive, or had she met some tragedy? Would I even recognize her if I saw her today? And if I did, what in the hell would I say to her?

Would she recognize me?

"Do you want to leave?" Kate asked.

"No."

When it started to pour, I stood and pulled Kate to her feet. "Come on," I said. "Everybody's going to wonder who the two strangers are that don't have sense enough to come in out of the rain."

Kate nodded and went inside first, squeezing into a spot against the back wall, close to the door. The people standing by us shuffled a few steps to their right to make room. I ended up right by the door so I could feel a breeze against my back. On the other side of the doorway was the man who had given up his seat. The pale gray of his suit made his blue eyes look so striking that I held his gaze entirely too long. When he smiled and nodded a greeting, I felt myself flush and quickly looked away. I was failing miserably at this incognito business.

Kate nudged me again as her lip curved ever so slightly upward.

I knew she was partly teasing, trying to put me at ease and make me think about anything besides my mother and Vergie.

I mouthed the word, *Stop*, and turned back to the preacher, who was thanking us all for coming out to celebrate Vergie on this dreary day.

THUNDER RUMBLED beneath the hymns as the rain went from

a soft patter to a roar. The lights flickered, but the preacher's voice rolled on with a rhythm so similar to undulating waves that it had to have been carefully rehearsed. Lightning crashed around us, filling the room with blue light. The little church seemed to shake with the force of it all. I swallowed hard as everyone stood for the preacher's last words.

I tugged on Kate's elbow and nodded toward the door. She winced as thunder crashed overhead.

"It's pouring," she said.

"Let's make a break before everybody gets chatty."

I couldn't see who was in the front pews, reserved for close family, and I didn't want to. We were jostled away from the open door as people moved to the front and greeted each other. I gently pushed my way toward the door but got intercepted by a lady in a dark blue skirt suit.

"Isn't this weather just awful?" she said, blocking my exit. She was holding a gardenia that was bursting from its tiny pot. Her hair was gray, with streaks as white as the flower's blooms.

I glanced behind me and saw Kate being nudged right into the path of the man in the light gray suit. A few seconds later, she was talking to him, smiling her megawatt smile. They both looked my way, and I turned my back to them.

When the lady with the gardenia stepped closer, the sweet scent filled the air between us, and I thought of Vergie, picking the same ruffled blossoms from her garden by the porch. When she cut a few for a vase, their scent had filled the whole house.

The woman cocked her head and said, "You must be Martine's daughter."

"Oh," I said. My throat tightened at the mention of my mother's name. "I'm just a—"

"You're the spitting image of her. Is she here? I haven't seen her in ages."

I stammered, but the words wouldn't come. I glanced toward the front of the church, looking for anyone else who looked like me, and felt a surge of panic.

"I'm Florie," she said, wrestling the plant so she could take my hand in hers.

"Nice to meet you," I said, my voice shaking.

She squeezed my hand and smiled, then thrust the gardenia at me. "Would you take this for the family?" she said. "I won't be able to wait in that long line. Tell them I'll just come by the house later."

"But I'm not—"

"Thank you, sugar," she said, and hobbled past me out the door. A young woman rushed up with an umbrella and walked her down the ramp to a waiting car.

I turned back to Kate and saw the preacher hugging a woman with dark brown hair pulled up in a bun. When she turned toward me, I held my breath. I stared at her, rooted in place, but shook the thought away when she turned to talk to someone else. *Pull it together*, I told myself. But then another woman about her age gave me a long hard stare, and I felt my heart clench like a fist. I'd thought many times about the day I might see my mother again. I'd imagined all the things I might say to her, then decided the chances of seeing her were too slim to give it any more attention.

But now it seemed all too likely. I turned and bolted out the door, holding the gardenia against my chest.

The rain was cold against my skin. I ran into the field in front of the church and stood in the grass, lightning streaking all around me. The sky was a charcoal gray, with not even a sliver of sunlight. I'd convinced myself that my mother had vanished entirely, and I'd accepted that as truth. The thought of bumping into her, having to speak to her, made me feel so sick I could barely breathe. Rain dripped down my arms and chest. I felt the warmth of tears and then heard Kate's voice over the rain.

"Hey!" she called. She wobbled over, her high heels sinking in the grass. Behind her, the man in the gray suit was standing in the doorway. He moved toward us like he might follow her, but an older man stepped up and shook his hand, grasping him by the shoulder. As he spoke to the older man, he kept looking our way like he might chase after us.

"Let's get out of here before we get struck by lightning," Kate said. She grabbed my elbow and steered me to the car. We walked quickly through the grass as the sky lit up all around us. She flinched as she opened my car door and the ground shook with thunder. All I felt was the cold of the rain as I glanced back at the church. Kate stared straight ahead, chewing on her fingernail. The rain hammered on the roof of the car.

"Let's just go," I said, tossing the floppy hat into the back seat. My head was starting to hurt, but the tears wouldn't stop.

I hated to cry.

"I can't see anything," Kate said. "Give it a few minutes."

Lightning flashed around us as a few people dashed for their cars. Most of them were still in the church, waiting out the rain. The sweetness of the gardenia filled the car.

"Please," I said, feeling my chest tighten. My mother was like a myth. I'd thought of her that way for so long that I'd never allowed myself to believe she could also be leading a perfectly average life somewhere else, not too far away even. And that she could cross paths with me at any point in time. Right then, I realized I *had* always thought of her as dead, because that was the only permanent *gone* I knew.

The other kinds of *gone* hurt a hell of a lot more. Other kinds of *gone* involved a choice.

"Enza," Kate said, nodding toward the church. "Do you think she was in there?"

"I don't know. I wouldn't know her if I saw her."

"Wouldn't you, though?"

I coughed as I fought back sobs, gripping the plant in my lap to stop my hands from shaking.

"Let's get out of here," I said. "Please, Kate. Even if we only go a mile."

She started the car and eased out of the grass and onto the gravel road that led back to the highway. The rain hit the windshield in sheets, so she drove slowly, both hands on the top of the wheel. Her brow was furrowed, her lips set in a hard line.

"I wish I'd known this about you," she said. "About your mother."

"I'd convinced myself she didn't exist any more," I said. "But what if she does?"

Kate's eyebrow arched as we skidded through a deep puddle and the car swerved. "Doesn't change anything," she said. "Once you get out of here, the chances of you seeing her are as slim as you want them to be."

Chapter Five

I set the gardenia in the window of our room at the Dauphine Inn and fell asleep thinking of summers with Vergie.

Kate lay sprawled in the bed next to mine, sleeping diagonally just because she could. She snored quietly between slow breaths.

Every time I closed my eyes, I saw Vergie's bright blue eyes and gray hair, the way her eyes had wrinkled at the corners when she smiled at me. I remembered her fishing in the lagoon behind her house, both of us rolling our jeans up to our knees, sitting on the dock so we could splash our feet in the water. She teased me, telling me a catfish would bite our toes if we didn't bait the hooks well enough. We'd pack sandwiches for lunch so we could stay out there all day. It was like escaping to a whole different world.

Sometime after two, I got up and crept out of the room, careful not to wake Kate. The inn had a courtyard with a small garden and a rock path. The wild roses and honeysuckle were so sweet I could almost taste them on my tongue. I lay in the grass for a long while, staring up at the stars. The sky was clear, but the moon was so bright it was hard to draw a line between the few constellations I could remember. Vergie had taught me some of them—Orion, Cassiopeia, Cygnus. I couldn't see much of anything in the sky in Raleigh, but out here she connected all the stars, dragging her finger through the air, telling me about heroes and goddesses, creatures I wished might protect me someday. She'd made everything seem magical. She'd made me feel like I was more than ordinary, and that was a feeling I'd long forgotten.

When I caught myself dozing off in the grass, I went back inside, opening the door softly. Kate rolled over when I shut the door, but she didn't wake. I pulled the sheet over me and breathed in the scent of gardenia, wishing I could go back to when I was sixteen and do just one thing differently.

IN THE BLUE-TINTED MOONLIGHT, I was walking through a field. The hay was high, up to my waist. I walked with my arms out beside me, letting the hay touch me as I moved along. An arm slipped around my waist, and then another pulled me close. I leaned back against a muscular frame, and those arms tightened around me, pulling me against a taut body that was familiar, but somehow not. I smiled as a stubbly cheek slid along my neck and lips grazed the curve of my jaw.

He whispered my name as his hands roamed over my hips, underneath the fabric of my dress. The light strokes of his fingers tickled my skin until his grip tightened, and I slid my hands along his forearms, wishing he would use them to lay me down in the grass.

He turned me toward him, cupping my face in his hands. He kissed me with a fierceness that made me shiver, and when I opened my eyes, I was startled by the intense blue of his eyes. His fingers traced a line along my shoulder, my ribs, as if committing the contours to memory. He slid his hands along my back, pulling me closer, and there was nowhere else I wanted to be.

I awoke with a jolt and sat up in bed. I looked to my left, thinking surely I wasn't alone, but there I was with the sheets twisted at my feet, the extra pillow tossed on the floor. The man from the funeral was not there, but I'd half expected him to be.

"What's the matter?" Kate asked. She was across the room, pulling on a pair of jeans. "Nightmare?"

"Not exactly," I said, feeling flushed.

I shook my head, trying to knock those thoughts right out of my brain. I could still feel the warmth of his hands, the way they had squeezed my hips when he kissed me. *Ridiculous*, I told myself, *having dreams about a man you saw for ten minutes.*

But I'd never had one that vivid before.

"Sex dream," Kate said.

I frowned.

She grinned, pointing her finger at me.

"You know, that's a really annoying habit you have," I said.

"You mean skill," she said. "A highly sought-after one, I might add."

"Let's just get some breakfast."

"Was it about Sexy Gray Suit Guy? He's excellent dream fodder."

"What if I said yes?"

"My grandma used to have psychic dreams," Kate said, grabbing her purse.

"It was not a psychic dream."

"How do you know?"

"Because I'll never see him again. I'll probably never see any of this again."

IN THE INN's dining room, mismatched antique chairs sat around small tables. Several places were set with china mixed and matched by color palette. We chose a table by the window, and I poured two cups of coffee into teacups with handles so tiny my fingers barely slipped into them.

"What should we do today?" Kate asked. She flinched at the chicory and added more milk.

"You're dying to go downtown, aren't you?" I said.

She raised her eyebrows, sipping her coffee. "I wouldn't mind being a tourist."

I stared out over the field, watching cows graze in the pasture beyond the inn.

"Let's go be tourists, then," I said. "Vergie took me all over, so she'd like it if I showed off her fair city to somebody else."

Chapter Six

I LET Kate drag me through all the boutiques in the Faubourg
Marigny district and even humored her by trying on a few
dresses. At the last shop, she wouldn't let me leave until I agreed
to buy a deep purple one with a halter top.

I'd tried it just to keep Kate quiet, but still I twirled in the
dressing room, just to watch the A-line skirt flare out at my
knees. I pulled my hair back from my face and thought it would
likely be a long time before I had an excuse to wear it, but every
now and then I got to dress like a woman. Usually it was for a
friend who was getting married, or some shindig with the local
historical society. I supposed it couldn't hurt to have a nice dress
waiting in the closet for the next big event.

"You should wear that kind of thing more often," Kate said
when I came out of the dressing room. "You could stop
traffic."

I shrugged. "It's all right."

She rolled her eyes. "You're not leaving here without that
dress. I don't care if it costs as much as your car payment."

I looked at the tag and said, "It *is* almost as much as my car payment."

Kate folded her arms over her chest. "One of these days, Enza, you're going to need a proper va-va-voom dress. It'd be criminal to let you walk out of here without that one."

WE HAD lunch on the square and sat outside, listening to a band play across the way. There was an upright bass, a violin and a keyboard—quite the backup for a singer on the square. They were playing old zydeco favorites as passersby dropped bills into an empty violin case.

When the waiter brought our drinks, something he called a "hummingbird" that had so much fruit juice we could barely taste the bourbon, I held my glass up and toasted. "To Vergie."

"To Vergie," Kate said, clinking her glass against mine. "I wish I'd been lucky enough to know her."

"I wish I'd known her better," I said, taking a sip. "Kate, thank you. For everything."

"Any time. You know that."

The band started into another tune, and one of the guys pulled out an accordion. We listened for a long while, watching the tourists come and go, snapping pictures as they paused by the fountain.

After lunch, we passed the band as we crossed the square, and the singer tipped his hat toward us.

"Hey," Kate said, grabbing my arm. "Let's get our future told."

I followed her gaze to where a woman draped in batik-dyed

fabric sat at a card table with a hand-painted sign that read *Palm
Readings.*

"Come on," she said. "It'll be fun."

Before I could protest, Kate trotted right up to the woman's
table and sat in the chair across from her. She motioned for me
to follow, but I was fixated on the band, the way the violinist
played with her eyes closed, moving her head in a quick,
staccato rhythm. She stood with her back against the singer, as if
performing for someone who wasn't there. She was tall and thin,
her hair cropped short.

When the song ended, a few tourists clapped and dropped
loose change into the violin case. I placed a five inside, then
went over to Kate.

Donita was the palm reader's name. She wore a pale yellow
dress and had her bright red hair piled on top of her head. She
looked more like a pin-up girl than a palm reader. She glanced
at me as I hovered next to Kate, then traced her finger along
Kate's palm.

"I see three great loves in your life," she said, tapping a
bright blue fingernail against her palm.

Kate raised an eyebrow. "What if I've already had three?
You saying it's all downhill for the rest of my life?"

Donita smiled. "That's the scientist part of you," she said.
"So literal. You haven't had three great ones yet."

"I know a couple of guys who would beg to differ."

Donita pointed to a line. "You've got to wait a little longer
on your best match. He shows up when this line crosses from
the Saturn mound over your heart line."

"You have an ETA on that?" Kate asked.

Donita smiled. "This next intersecting line is at about age forty, so somewhere before that."

Kate frowned.

"Could meet him in two years or two days," Donita said. "We have to make ourselves available to the universe for new opportunities."

Kate shook her head. That was a little too mystical for her taste. She usually called that kind of talk "woo-woo" and rolled her eyes.

"Fair enough," she said. "My friend Enza here needs a turn."

I started to protest, but Kate jumped up from the chair and practically shoved me into it.

"Hi. I'm Enza."

I reached out to shake Donita's hand, but she took my wrist and turned my palm up. "Nice to meet you," she said, and studied my hand.

As she traced her finger over the lines of my palm, she mentioned that I worked with my hands, that I had serious grief in my childhood, that I kept myself guarded because of it. I sat stone faced, not wanting to give her any leading answers, but I was certain she was telling me things she told a dozen other people every day. It's not hard to look at someone and pin her for an introvert, or a tomboy; it's equally easy to identify someone who uses her hands for manual labor. I was certainly no mystery to a woman who studied strangers all day, and I didn't pretend to be surprised by her "insights." I'd play along for Kate, though, because it was obvious she was trying to take my mind off my mother and Vergie.

"You're leaving soon," Donita said, and I thought, *Duh, just like every other tourist you see on the square.*

"But you're not finished here," she said. "You'll be back soon."

"This is my last visit here," I said, smiling. "This was a trip to tie up loose ends, and I think we've done it."

Kate winked at me. Donita tapped her fingernail against my lifeline.

"See the way this little line runs alongside it?" she said. "It almost forms a chain pattern. Each time it crosses the lifeline is a time you'll come back, a time of great significance."

I leaned down so closely to look that our heads were nearly touching. The looping pattern started close to my thumb. There was a break in the chain, and then the loops appeared again near the middle of my palm.

"You've come here already many times," she said, "but then there's a break of ten to fifteen years, and then you start coming back. Then the lifeline splits—very unusual. That signifies a great change that has the potential to put you on a very different path than the one you were on."

I glanced at Kate. She raised her eyebrows and shrugged.

I pulled my hand away and stood.

"Well, thanks, Donita," I said.

She looked at me, her green eyes wide. "Don't you want to hear the rest?"

"Nah." I pulled some cash from my purse and handed it to her. "I like to have a few surprises."

Chapter Seven

FOR THE DURATION of the flight home, I had to hold the gardenia in my lap. I'd hoped it might ride in an empty seat between me and Kate, but the flight was full. I sat squished against the window, Kate at my elbow. The bald man next to her sneezed through most of the flight, making Kate wince each time. We agreed that until we got back to Raleigh, we would not talk about (a) my mother, (b) my father, or (c) what I'd do with my life if I quit working for my father.

"Maybe I can find you a Sexy Gray Suit Guy back home," Kate said at last.

"I think maybe I need a break from the dating pool."

"That's just silly," she said. "Now I know your type."

I rolled my eyes. "I don't have a type."

"I'll have to line a few up before next month, though."

"What's the rush?"

She flipped through her magazine and held it up like a shield when the man next to her sneezed again.

"I have to go out of town for a few weeks. The lab's sending me to a training session in Denver."

"A few weeks?"

"Eight," she said.

"Wow," I said. "That sounds big time."

"It would make me eligible for a promotion," she said.

"Who will I have cocktails with while you're gone?"

She grinned. "That's what I'm trying to arrange."

I shook my head, picking at the dead leaves on the gardenia. "Not the same. There's no stunt double befitting you."

"Just wait until I find you a nice carpenter with steady hands and a deep-seated need to please."

The bald man sneezed.

THERE WAS a sliver of moon that night, high in the sky. It was difficult to make out the stars with all the street lights in my neighborhood, but I convinced myself I'd found the Big Dipper, tracing my finger along imaginary lines between stars, the way Vergie once did. I listened to a voicemail from my father, instructing me to go back to the almost-frat-house in the morning, and then went out to the garage to find my shovel.

Even though it was well after ten, the horizon still had an orange cast to it from all the lights in town. I hadn't realized how perpetually bright it was here until I'd laid out in the grassy field at the Dauphine, staring up at a darkness that felt like it could pull me up inside it at any moment. Now it seemed strange to have so much light at night, to have no real darkness.

I dug a hole in the yard by the back porch, about eight

inches across and eight inches deep. The ground was mostly clay after the first few inches, and I had to jump on the shovel to cut through. When it was finally deep enough, I filled the hole with water and waited for it to drain. Before I'd set foot back in Bayou Sabine, I'd told myself that was going to be my last visit there. My memories of that place had held so much hurt that I'd pushed them away for as long as I could remember. I'd convinced myself there was nothing left for me there and no reason to ever return. But going back had made me see how wrong I was about that. I had cut out a significant portion of my life, and it might be too late to do anything about it.

But it might not.

I'd been afraid to stand up to my father back then. Afraid to ask for what I wanted. Afraid to push for what I thought was right. I would not make that mistake again.

I placed the gardenia in the hole and packed the dirt around it, soaking it again to compact the soil. The ruffled white blooms glowed in the darkness, and I smiled, thinking of how Vergie had spread so much goodness in the world around her. I hated that I wouldn't know more about her, but I figured I could at least adopt a few of her finer habits.

At the edge of the backyard was the pickup truck holding the pallet full of daylilies and hostas. I'd watered them before I left with Kate, and they'd managed to survive a few days in the heat without me. I smiled, thinking of how good they'd look alongside the porch at the Durham house, and tossed the shovel into the truck.

It was darker in the historic district but not by much. I could hear a radio on in the house next door, some people laughing on a porch across the street. I straightened the "for sale" sign and set my flashlight on the porch, aimed out into the yard. I started at the corner of the flower bed the landscaper had laid out and dug holes along the porch railing eighteen inches apart. I'd put compost down before Dad had intercepted me and stopped my beautification of the saddest yard on the block. That, however, was before he told me about Vergie's death. Before I saw his cold expression when he talked about her.

Before I realized there was a lot he'd hidden from me.

I dug through the compost, thinking of the last summer at Vergie's I could remember. I'd been fifteen and boy crazy, and Vergie was trying to get me to concentrate on anything but boys. She'd hired a lady down the street to give me piano lessons, which had kept me occupied only on the hottest afternoons.

My shirt was sticking to my back, but still I dug.

The voices on the porch quieted.

A woman jogged past with a Golden Retriever, its coat gleaming in the pale light.

I heard the katydids buzzing in the cypresses, smelled the salt in the air and split the earth with the shovel.

My fingers burned where the wood handle rubbed old calluses, but still I dug.

I thought of Mike, how he so easily won my father over, and pushed the blade of the shovel into the loamy soil.

I filled the holes with water, then set the lilies out, alternating yellow and orange along the front of the porch. This would prove that something could thrive here, that this was a home that would foster growth. As I packed the dirt around the last lily, I inhaled, drawing in the scent of the earth. When I held my hands out in front of me, the lines in my palms were more visible, darkened by the soil. I traced the lines with my fingers, and I gazed at the life line that Donita said would lead me back to Bayou Sabine. I thought of my father, the way he'd react when he saw this yard full of lilies, the way he'd use this as something else to hold against me. I thought of how my memories weren't as distant as I'd once believed and understood that this was not a goodbye to Vergie. This was not an ending.

I waved to the neighbors on the porch across the street as I walked into the yard and sat in the grass. The lilies were bright under the moon, glowing in the beam of the flashlight. I brushed the dirt from the palms of my hands and leaned back on my elbows. The grass tickled my skin, and I breathed deeply, taking in as much of the night as I could, and for a moment, wished that it might rain.

Want more of the Bayou Sabine series?

Bayou Sabine isn't done with Enza Parker just yet. Her story continues in *Bayou My Love*, when Enza is drawn back to the town that holds so many secrets of her past, and so much promise for the future she dreams of. In Bayou Sabine, she collides with the most alluring man she's ever met—and finds another that will bring certain disaster.

Here is the opening of the novel.

Bayou My Love: A Bayou Sabine Novel

Chapter 1

I knew when I strode into my father's office—before he'd had time to drink his two cups of coffee—that I was asking for trouble. But I was furious.

He glared at me, the phone cradled to his ear. His upper lip twitched in the way that usually sent people running with fear. As I sat down in the chair across from his desk, I could hear the muffled voice on the other end of the line. Judging by the way he scribbled on his notepad, nearly piercing the paper, the conversation wasn't going well. If I were a more dutiful daughter, and less hacked off at him, I might have come back later. But he'd been ignoring me all week. I needed a straight answer about my next job and was tired of waiting.

My father has a knack for taking roughed-up houses and making them look like they belong in the glossy pages of architectural magazines. I'd started working for him when I was in college and discovered I had a knack for it too.

This fact puts him in a tough spot. On the one hand, he'd like his progeny to take over his company one day. On the other hand, his progeny is me: a hard-headed thirty-one-year-old woman whose general presence aggravates his ulcers. I don't do things the way he does, and he's a control freak. This often puts us at an impasse.

Most of our jobs work out OK. Because I get bored easily, the short-lived challenge of a new house-flip appeals to me. My father sleeps a little easier when his daughter has steady employment and is not too close to his office. He likes to micromanage me, though, and that's where things get hairy.

Still on the phone, he leaned back in his prized Mission-style chair and shook his hand at me to say *shoo*. I crossed my arms over my chest and raised my brows. He pointed to the door more emphatically. I propped my feet on his desk.

His eyes narrowed as they rested on my beat-up cowboy boots. They were my favorite pair, vintage brown and white with tulip and bluebird inlays. He grimaced whenever I wore them and called them unprofessional. In the beginning, he'd expected me to dress more like a real estate agent, in a nice skirt suit with heels. But skirt suits were completely against my nature. I was a tomboy through and through, perfectly happy in my jeans and plaid shirts. I usually took five minutes to pull my hair back in a ponytail and could sometimes be bothered to put on a little mascara, but that was the extent of my preening. My curvy figure and wildly curly hair had made for an unkind sprint through adolescence. My father was of no help in feminine matters, and my mother was long gone, so I'd fumbled my way through my formative years and came out the other side with zero appreciation for makeup or fashion. Heels put me just over six feet tall, and even though I had my mother's soft face, I intimidated most men.

It seemed more beneficial to focus on beautifying houses.

"I'll get somebody else over there immediately," my father said, slamming the phone down. He turned to me. "Honestly, it just can't get any crazier around here. I hope you're not coming in to tell me you're quitting too."

"I've been thinking about Grandma Vergie's house," I said.

"Enza, I don't have room for that on my plate right now. We'll get to it in a few months."

"I know you don't. That's why I have the perfect solution."

He stared at me over his glasses.

"What if I went down there myself and handled it?"

He chuckled like I'd told him a joke that wasn't all that funny.

When Vergie died a couple of months ago, she'd unexpectedly left her house to me. Dad suggested flipping it, despite my suggestion to keep it as a rental or a vacation home.

It was on a stream in southeast Louisiana, just a little north of New Orleans. Bayou Sabine was a beautiful area, but my father scoffed at the idea of another property to maintain. He wanted to turn it around as fast as possible. There was no room in his heart for nostalgia.

"I'm serious," I said. "I want to handle this one."

"Your first flip should be local."

"I've been doing this for years. Give me a chance."

The phone rang again, and he answered before I could finish. "Hang on a sec," he said into the phone. To me he said, "You can take the next one."

I was so tired of hearing that line. I'd been patient, doing all the dirty work he handed me for five years now. House after house, he'd had me doing clean-up and demo, filling dumpsters with all the garbage left from houses that had been auctioned. We were based out of Raleigh, a city where a lot of houses went to auction. Most days, I felt like I needed a haz-mat suit, because people who left pissed off or in a hurry, well, they weren't concerned with what they left behind. Piles of dirty clothes, rotting garbage, refrigerators that had reached DEFCON 1— nothing surprised me any more. Some days I thought he was making me do the grunt work just to scare me off. He knew I had a weak stomach for filth. What he didn't know was that there was no way I'd give him the satisfaction of seeing me fail.

My father delighted in watching failure.

Occasionally he'd toss me a compliment and say I had a good eye for architecture, or I had more patience than he did— but he still couldn't let me loose. Sure, he loved me, but sometimes it felt like he was trying to make me prove I was in this business to stay. He considered training me an investment, and his investments needed to bring returns. Turning my grandmother's house around would go a long way toward making him see me as more of a professional and less of a wayward daughter.

When I stood, he didn't shift his gaze to me. I reached over and held my finger down on the phone, breaking the connection on the line.

"Enza!" he yelled. "That was a contractor!"

"I don't want to wait for the next crummy house in the wrong part of town. This one's important."

"That sort of sentimentality is going to cost you a fortune," he said. "And by extension, cost me a fortune."

"This isn't about sentimentality."

He sighed, tapping his pen on the desk. "It's nothing but a swamp down there," he said. "The house won't be like you remember." He had a strange look on his face, one I couldn't quite decipher. Usually I could read my father well, because he's a straightforward guy and doesn't have time for things like subtext. This look wasn't anger or fear, exactly, but he was definitely hiding something.

I shook it off, focused on winning him over. "I still want to go," I said.

It had been years since I'd been down to that little corner of Louisiana. When I was a kid, I spent summers with Vergie. But when I was sixteen, shortly after Mom left (no one ever told me why, and eventually I gave up asking), my father told me there would be no more summers with Vergie. *She doesn't want you to visit any more,* he said flatly. Being a teenager, thinking the world hated me, I took that to mean Vergie hated me too.

It never occurred to me until years later that my father might have lied.

Sure, I could have sought Vergie out. But part of me believed my father and thought she really didn't want to see me. After all, she was my mom's mother. They had the same blood. Could they not have the same tendency to abandon me for no reason? I was scared that if I did go to see her, she'd turn me away and confirm everything my father said.

I couldn't take that kind of hurt again.

Years passed, and I shoved those memories to the back of my brain. I hardly thought of Vergie.

But then she died. Alone, for all I knew. And then I hated myself for not visiting her. Dad wouldn't even go to the funeral with me. I stood in the back of the church because I didn't want everyone talking to me like I knew her so well, her only grandchild. The little chapel was packed with people—easily a hundred—all fanning themselves in the heat. The whole time I felt like an impostor, and I had a headache for days from the tears. I didn't go to her house because I knew all those people would be there, swapping stories over dinner. I couldn't bear hearing all the things about her I'd missed out on.

We didn't find out until weeks later that she'd left the house to me. I thought the lawyers were mistaken, but it was true. And that made me feel worse than anything.

Dad was probably right to want to sell it—when would I ever be down there? The truth was, I didn't care about flipping it to turn a profit. I felt like I owed her: Repairing her house would be a kind of homage. The potential profit was just a way to get my father on board and let me use his resources.

Besides, it would do me good to get out of town for a while and go back to a place that had good memories tied to it.

My father's eyes narrowed. "You aren't going to go down there and get all attached are you? We don't have time for nostalgia."

"I want to turn this house around just as fast as you do."

"Then you won't have a hard time parting with it," he said, pushing his glasses up on his nose. With his gelled hair and oxford shirt, he looked like he belonged more on a used car lot than in a remodeling business. "I know you like to hang onto things that need fixing," he said, his eyebrow arched.

True, I took in strays. I dated men who were broken, hoping to mend their fatal flaws. Everyone has one, of course, but while my father chose to write people off because of their flaws, I urged my partners to overcome them. I took a lot of risks and failed more than I succeeded (with men, not renovations), but there's a science there, right? A law of averages. You fail enough, you succeed in the long run. Dad liked to hold this habit over my head. He wanted me to settle down with a reliable guy who could balance his checkbook and pay a mortgage on time. But every time I sought out reliable, it backfired. My last boyfriend had been a banker, but then he quit to be a writer. I'd let him stay with me, rent-free, while he tried to build up a freelance business, burning through his savings. I thought I was being supportive, but my father called him a moocher. When we finally broke up, my father said, *See what a waste of time and money that was?*

My father thought my propensity to fix people was a weakness. But he thought my inclination to fix houses was lucrative.

Houses were easy because you figure out what's broken, add the cost of materials plus the cost of labor, then factor in a little patience over time. Unlike men, renovations were something I could calculate.

"You said yourself you've got too much going on up here," I said. "Besides, we'll have squatters if we wait too long."

He stared for a long moment, then leaned back in his chair. Those were the magic words. My father despised freeloaders. "Fine. I'll give you six weeks. That should be plenty of time for that house."

"Six weeks," I said, wondering if he would actually trust me to finish on my own. A perfectionist to the core, he loved to show up halfway through a project and take over completely, arguing that his way was more cost-effective, more efficient. I hated that about him. Sometimes it was easier on everybody if he just came into the project in the beginning. It would save me a car load of aspirin and whiskey. But I was hoping this time he would leave me alone.

"This will give you the chance to see if you love this job as much as you think you do," he said, chewing on the tip of his pen.

I wanted it to spill blue ink down his lip.

"And this way you get to be the boss." He winked, then circled a day on his calendar. "Now, let's get your flight booked."

"Fair enough," I agreed. "But no planes—I'll drive."

He frowned and gave me a look of zero faith. "Right out the gate, wasting time."

"Saving money," I said. "No rental car."

"Try to stay focused down there, will you? Don't get distracted by anything else that needs fixing."

"Will do."

He reached for the phone and said, "Would you excuse me so I can get back to work here?" He was already dialing before I got to the door.

I stopped. "Why do you think she left the house to me?"

He sighed and laid his glasses on the desk. "Who could ever explain Vergie? She was nutty as a fruitcake." There was that unreadable look again. What was he hiding?

"I'll call when I get there, Dad."

"Bonne chance," he said, arching that eyebrow again. "You're gonna need all the luck you can get."

The door slammed behind me. I didn't need luck, and I was going to prove it.

∾

Cranking the radio up was the perfect antidote for a conversation with my father. I couldn't carry a tune in a bucket, but I figured that's why they made car radios—so people like me can blow off steam while driving through four states that look exactly alike and try to forget our fathers' lack of faith in us.

I'd spent the night somewhere in east Mississippi, in a motel that served moon pies and instant coffee as continental breakfast. It was a blessing I was exhausted when I checked in —I didn't notice much about the place and was able to sleep the peaceful slumber of a person ignorant of potential health hazards. Ordinarily, I wouldn't stay in a place like the Teddy Bear Motel, but around midnight, I'd finally gotten too tired to keep driving. It was the only place around. So I'd stripped the comforter off the bed, skipped the shower and brushed my teeth quickly, not staring too hard at the sink or counter. Too much scrutiny of that place and I'd itch all the way to Bayou Sabine.

A little after noon, it was already scorching. I cursed myself for not getting the Jeep's air conditioning fixed back in the spring. With the windows down, I tried to convince myself the heat wasn't so bad, but my clothes were sticking to me. The land around me had shifted from rolling hills to marshland, and at last I felt like I was out of my father's orbit. I was thinking less of him and more about those summers I'd spent at the big blue house on the bayou, Vergie teaching me to play poker while we sat on the porch. Starting in grade school, I'd visit her for nearly three months every June when school let out. It was my favorite time of the year. I could run around barefoot and go swimming in the creek at night, and I didn't have to be ladylike—ever. With Vergie, life seemed more magical. Anything was possible when I was with her.

As I opened the last moon pie I'd smuggled from the motel, I was hit with a flash from years before.

Vergie and I were sitting on a quilt in one of the old cemeteries, back in a corner under an oak tree with limbs that undulated along the ground like tentacles. She was telling me ghost stories while we had tea and beignets, the powdered sugar clinging to our noses. We sat still as tombstones while a funeral procession passed, the people dancing as music filled the whole sky.

"Why are those people having such a good time?" I asked. "Isn't that a funeral?"

"That's the grandest way you can say goodbye to someone," Vergie said.

Vergie's own funeral had been tame compared to the scene that day, and now I felt bad that we hadn't given her a send-off like that one. She would have appreciated that, and I would have remembered if I hadn't stayed away so long.

Why had it taken me fifteen years to come back?

I turned my thoughts back to the house as I crossed the state line. Six weeks wasn't much time.

I pulled off the interstate onto a smaller highway. From there on, the roads would get narrower until they carried me into the little community of Bayou Sabine. I vaguely remembered the way, but with all the canals out here, the roads start to look the same. It's beautiful—don't get me wrong—but if you were to turn me around three times and plop me down in the middle of this marshland, I'd likely never see North Carolina again.

I checked the GPS on my phone, but the road wasn't showing up.

"Oh, come on," I said, swiping my thumb across the screen. The red dot that was supposed to be me was now off the nearest named road. According to the GPS, I was in a bayou. I glanced up at the road, trying to get my bearings and not swerve into the water for real.

Signal lost, it said. I groaned, restarting the app. When I looked up, an alligator was lumbering across the road—all six feet of him stretched across my lane.

"Oh, hell!" I slammed the brake to the floor, flinching as the tires squealed and the Jeep fish-tailed. I bit my lip so hard I tasted blood, and I called that gator everything but a child of

God. I expected to hear a terrible thud at any second. Swerving, I missed him by just a few inches, but I was close enough to see his catlike eye as I shot across the opposite lane and onto the shoulder. Off to my left, there was nothing but swamp and black mud. I gripped the wheel, fighting to stay on the hard ground.

The Jeep stopped on what felt like solid earth, the weeds as high as the door handle. My heart hammered in my chest. Vergie used to tell me old voodoo legends about alligators, how they were tricksters, always causing trouble.

Please don't be stuck. Not out here.

My foot eased the gas pedal down, and the Jeep inched forward. The tires spun as I pushed harder. "This is not happening."

A rusty pickup rumbled toward me. The driver gave me a long look, but he hardly slowed down. I nudged the Jeep into four wheel drive and turned the tires as I hit the gas. It rocked a few times, then lurched forward and caught hold of the grass before crossing onto the pavement. I glanced back to where the alligator had crossed, but it was gone.

"Welcome back," I muttered to myself.

The old two-lane highway cut the land in half, with swamps on one side and pastures on the other. With the black water so close, I felt like the earth might open up and devour me at will. The trees were full of moss, the water creeping up their trunks like it was swallowing them.

I passed Vergie's driveway the first time, not recognizing it until I caught a glimpse of the pale blue goose she'd left by the mailbox like a sentinel. The paint was peeling, but the goose stood firmly in a patch of daylilies, just as it had since I was a girl. I turned around and eased onto the dirt drive. I felt the hollow in my chest expand, the void Vergie had left.

Cypress trees lined the road to the house, their limbs curling toward the ground. The breeze tickled the drooping leaves of the trees, and in the distance I heard the faint clink of glass, like a wind chime. Just beyond the house stood a spirit tree, bottles hanging from its branches like Christmas ornaments. It had been there long before Vergie, but she had added a few herself after drinking pints of bourbon and gin. She used to tell me those bottles captured evil spirits, kept them from roaming through the bayou and attaching themselves to good folks that lived nearby. I'd never really believed they held ghosts, but I liked the sound of the wind whistling over the lips of the bottles. Now, as the light glinted blue and green in the leaves of the tree, the sound felt more melancholy than soothing.

This place had a wildness that was hard not to like. It smelled sweet like magnolia, bitter like the swamp. Egrets dotted the trees like blooms of cotton, preening themselves in the slivers of sunlight. The driveway wound back into the woods, hidden from the main road. Patches of gravel mixed with the soil, packed hard from the heat and drought. When at last I pulled into the yard, I was surprised at how small the house seemed compared to my memory of it. It was still plenty big at two stories high, but it was a paler shade of blue than I remembered, and the roof was missing some shingles. The porch was cluttered with potted flowers, strings of lights hanging from the eaves, and a hammock strung between two corner posts. I could almost see Vergie's silhouette in the rocker, and I knew then that I was going to prove my father wrong.

I had to. I owed it to Vergie. This place was a part of her, and it was a part of me now too. I had to do this right.

It wasn't until I saw a pair of feet dangling from the hammock that I noticed the truck parked under a tree at the edge of the yard. A small dark pickup with patches of rust like spots on a horse. I squinted at the feet, thinking surely I was seeing something that wasn't there. But there was no mistaking the shape in the hammock, the lazy swinging motion.

I leapt from the car and slammed the door so hard that a head rose above the banister. My father had dealt with squatters once or twice, but I hadn't thought they'd move in so fast. Striding toward the steps, I cursed myself for not coming by when I was in town for the funeral.

I tried to cool my temper and concentrated on the sound of my boot heels pounding the dirt. There was no turning back now, because the man had definitely seen me.

He sat up in the hammock, and I swallowed hard as I reached the steps.

Chapter 2

THE MAN'S HAIR WAS RUMPLED, as if he'd slept in that hammock all night. His shirt, rolled at the wrists, was pushed up just enough from his pants that I could see a thin band of tan skin above his belt. He appeared to be only a few years older than me, but had tiny wrinkles around his eyes and lips that suggested he'd spent more time in the sun. And he looked familiar. My mind raced, trying to figure out where I'd seen him before.

"Hi there," he said, sitting up straight. "Are you lost?"

"No," I said, planting my hands on my hips. *Be calm,* I thought. *This doesn't have to get ugly.*

"I don't get too many visitors. I figured you took a wrong turn off the main road. You'd have to be lost to end up out here." His drawl made my ears tingle in a nice way, but the way he lounged in the hammock like he owned the place made me want to push him out of it head first.

"How about you tell me who you are," I said. "And what you're doing here."

He sat up straighter, running his hands through his dark hair. It was short, but stood out in tufts, as if the wind had pulled it through the holes in the hammock. "I believe it's customary for the interloper to identify herself to the current inhabitant," he said, half-smiling. "Not the other way around."

"This is my house," I said, trying to hold my temper down. "So that makes you the interloper."

He chuckled. "Darlin', I think you've got me confused with somebody else that lives in the middle of nowhere. Who are you looking for?" His tone was even, as if this kind of encounter happened every week.

"I'm not looking for a who," I said. "I'm looking for a house. This house. And last I checked, I didn't have any long-lost cousins living in it."

He glanced around him. "Well, one of us is in the wrong place. And it ain't me." His dark blue eyes held me in a warm gaze that in any other situation would make me want to lean in closer.

"This is my grandmother's house," I said, no longer caring when or where I might have seen him before. The priority was my property.

He cocked his head. "You mean Vergie?" His eyes lit up. "Well, why didn't you say so, darlin'?" He eased out of the hammock as slow as a river. Even his voice swaggered, and I imagined what it would sound like against my ear.

I shook my head to erase the thought.

When he stood, he smoothed his shirt down against his body. Tall and muscular, he towered over me, and I'm no small woman. His shirt was snug against his broad shoulders, pulled taut across his biceps. He held out his hand, smiling like I was some long lost friend, and in spite of myself, I shook it.

"I'm Jack Mayronne," he said. His big hand squeezed mine, and I swallowed hard as something that felt like static electricity rippled down my arm.

"Enza Parker," I said, struggling to keep my voice firm. "You knew my grandmother?" The nagging feeling returned. Where had I seen him? At this house when I was a teenager? Recently, when I was back for the funeral? I'd blocked so many of those images from my mind, and right now was not the time to try to recover them.

His thumb slid along my palm, and I saw a tattoo peeking out from under the sleeve of his shirt, a black curve like a snake. I wondered how far up it went.

"Sure," he said, holding my hand a little too long. "She was a fine lady. And if you come from that stock, I guess you're all right."

"That still doesn't explain what you're doing in her house."

He grinned, shoving his hands into his pockets. He looked like he could have come from a rodeo, in his faded jeans and plaid pearl-snap shirt. "You're just as feisty as she was, aren't you? I always liked that about her."

I felt my cheeks redden, and I hoped he didn't notice. Maybe he'd think it was the heat. After all, summer in Louisiana feels like being inside an oven.

"I've been renting this place for several months now," he said. A dog crossed the yard and trotted over. It lifted one ear toward the sound of Jack's voice and then sat by his feet. "Hey, jolie," he said, bending down to pat her on the head. She was stocky, and speckled brown and gray like granite, with expressive ears and a docked tail. Her eyes narrowed in my direction, and she let out a half-hearted bark.

"A Catahoula," I said, holding my hand out for her to sniff.

"Yeah," Jack said, and she snorted.

"The lawyer never mentioned anyone renting this house," I said.

"Probably didn't know. Vergie had only been living in the city for about six months. She let me stay here for practically nothing, just so it wouldn't sit empty."

"In the city?"

"She was staying in New Orleans with a friend," he said, still stroking the dog's fur. "Didn't you know?"

"We were out of touch for a long time."

"I was awful sad to hear about her," he said. "They broke the mold when they made Vergie."

It bothered me that he knew more about my own grandmother than I did. And it hurt when I thought about how

I'd avoided this place for so long, how I'd gone so many years without seeing the woman who had been like a second mother to me. I pushed the regrets away to stop my voice from cracking. "I spent every summer here when I was a kid," I said, sitting down next to him on the porch steps.

Ordinarily, I wouldn't let my guard down with a stranger, but the drive and the humidity had left me weak. With no breeze, the air was stifling, and I was grateful for any patch of shade.

"Me, too," he said. "I mean, I used to work for her. Started when I was about seventeen."

"Really?"

"Yard work and odd jobs. She was trying to keep me out of trouble, I think."

I smiled, wondering if that was true.

"Strange," he said. "We could have met years ago. Wouldn't that be something?" He stared at me for a while, like he might recognize me.

Maybe that was it... I glanced away.

The dog pressed her nose against my thigh. She squinted at me and then dropped her head on my knee as I scratched her ears.

"You all right?" he asked. "You look a little pale." He set those eyes on me again, and I felt like I'd burn up right there on the porch. He seemed to genuinely care, despite the fact that I'd accused him of trespassing.

"It's the heat," I said. "I'm not used to it any more."

He smiled, revealing dimples that were made for disarming people like me. "Where are you coming from?"

"Raleigh." My eyes drifted to the inside of his forearm, to his tattoo. I had a soft spot for tattoos—especially the kind only partially revealed by clothing. I didn't want him to catch me staring, though, so I looked back to the dog, who had started to drool on my knee. Apparently she'd decided I was no longer a threat.

"How about a glass of water?" he asked, touching my arm.

"Sure, thanks."

He stared at me like he thought I might faint. "It's a hot one today. I'd bring you inside, but the A/C units have been acting up, blowing fuses every chance they get. I'm trying to give them a rest."

I leaned against the stair railing, feeling light-headed.

"At least out here there's a breeze," he said. He disappeared into the house, leaving me on the porch. I pictured myself sitting in a rocker with Vergie, sipping tea and eating macaroons. It didn't seem possible that someone else could live here now.

"Here you go, chère," Jack said, sitting next to me again.

chère. I fought back a smile, thinking that was likely his way of getting anything he wanted from a woman. There probably weren't many that could turn down the likes of him.

Jack's knee brushed mine, and I instinctively moved my leg away. "You know you have to leave," I said. I tried to be as nice as possible while standing my ground. Being a landlord was not anywhere on my to-do list.

"Usually it takes longer for women to tell me that."

"Sorry," I told him. "I'm no good at evicting people."

"Then don't," he said, his voice light. He smiled again.

"I'm not in the business of renting. I'm here to fix this house and sell it. I'm afraid that means you have to leave."

"But I live here," he said. "You know how hard it is to find nice places out this way?"

"Didn't you think that when the landlady died, you should start looking for a new house?" I leaned against the banister, fanning myself. "I'm sorry that this comes as a surprise to you, but I've got no other option."

He shrugged. "I'd paid Miss Vergie up through the next few months. I figured I had a couple more weeks to worry about moving."

I tried to wrap my head around the logic of that. It was hard to give him a firm glare when he gazed at me with those woeful eyes.

Like a calf in a hailstorm, Vergie would have said.

"How about if I refund your rent?"

He ran his hands through his hair. "How about you keep renting to me," he suggested.

I laughed but then saw he was serious. "I'm no landlord, Mr. Mayronne. I don't have time for that kind of responsibility."

"How hard can it be, chère? You just collect a check now and then."

"I don't live around here. I can't keep this place up."

"I've been keeping it up just fine." He sounded insulted. "You think I called Miss Vergie every time a pipe burst? I've been fixing things up all the while. You wouldn't need to be nearby."

The place did look OK, but he'd done some half-assed repairs. A couple of boards on the porch were unfinished, recently replaced. The paint on the door and window sills was fresher than the rest, making the older paint look dirty. The inside was probably peppered with spots that needed a matching coat of paint or a few finishing nails. People were constantly doing do-it-yourself repairs only halfway, which always meant more work for me.

"You'll have to find another place," I said.

The dog sat up, ears flat.

"But Enza, you can't just kick me out." His eyes were bright blue, but they flashed darker as he became flushed. When the light hit them, I saw little flecks of green, and I wanted to lean in for a better look. I was helpless around good-looking, charming guys like him, and I knew if he caught on to that, he'd try anything to stay.

I set the glass of water on the ground and stood so I could glare down at him. "I'm the owner, Mr. Mayronne. I can do whatever I want." He might have been a friend of Vergie's, but that didn't mean he'd have her roof over his head for the rest of his life.

The dog growled, deep in her throat, and wiggled her haunches. Jack pointed a finger at her, and she stopped. "Come on, chère," he said. "I don't want any trouble. But I don't want to be out of a home, either."

"Look, this isn't personal. This is running a business."

He stood then, rising a head higher than me. "This is not what your grandmother would want," he said calmly.

I climbed to the top step to look him in the eye again. "How would you know what she'd want?" I leaned closer. "How dare you."

"Because she was thoughtful and considerate," he said, standing so close I could see those stupid green flecks in his eyes, "and she wouldn't kick a man out into the cold."

"I don't think you have to worry about the cold around here."

He leaned against the banister. "I signed a lease, you know. I'm supposed to have a few months left."

"There's a loophole for death of the landlord. Those are standard." I glared at him until he finally looked away.

He paced across the porch. His broad shoulders drooped as he shoved his hands in his pockets. I felt bad for the guy, but there wasn't an easy way out of this. As Jack Mayronne scratched his stubbly chin, he reminded me of the last man I fell in love with. He used to scratch his chin like that when he was deep in thought. I could still feel the roughness of his cheek against my skin. The thought made me shiver.

I shoved the thought away. Right now I needed to focus on fixing this house and proving my father was wrong about me. *You've got no follow-through, Enza,* he liked to say all too often. I told myself that was just boredom—if I could finish projects fast enough, then I wouldn't push details aside. Even though Dad was a big-picture man, he loved zooming in on the details and using them to point out my weaknesses.

I hated him for that, but I feared he might be right. Fixing this house, though, would prove I wasn't as weak-willed as he liked to think. That would be one delicious moment.

But first I had to get rid of this man who seemed as rooted here as the cypress in the backyard.

"Surely we can come to some kind of agreement," he said.

"Yes. You can leave as soon as possible."

"How long will it take you to fix this place up like you want it?"

I studied the peeling paint, the hedges that were overtaking the rails. "What difference does that make?"

"Come on. Humor me."

"I couldn't say without seeing the inside."

"So let's take a tour." He pushed the front door open and motioned for me to go in. The dog raced through ahead of us.

Before I could argue, he led me inside by the elbow. He could easily bash me over the head, but if I wanted to see the house, my options were limited. This seemed to be the only peaceful way. And I felt it would be a mistake to get him angry. People often get defensive about their homes, and I needed to stay on Jack Mayronne's good side.

"How about you let me stay—just while you fix things up," he said. "That should give me enough time to find another place."

I barely heard him as we walked down the hallway into the kitchen. I saw myself at twelve years old, sitting at the table playing checkers with Vergie, both of us wearing frilly old dresses, sipping imaginary mint juleps and fanning ourselves with antique lace fans. The room was plainer now, with straight lace sheers over the windows. But the old table and chairs remained.

"Most of her stuff is still here," he said. "She rented it furnished, and I travel light."

I felt a pang of guilt. How could I not know she was living some place other than her home?

"So you're Martine's daughter, then?" he asked.

I stopped. "How do you know my mother?"

He turned toward me, biting his lip like he wished he could

take those words back, then said, "Just from Vergie talking about her sometimes."

The thought of him knowing about my mother left me dumbstruck. I followed him through the house in a trance, sorting out what was real and what was not.

He led me through the living room, the back bedroom and the sitting room, and I tried to remember the last time I talked to Vergie. The few times I'd prodded my father to explain why I couldn't see her any more, he had quickly changed the subject. After my mother left, the summer visits had stopped. Why had I cut all ties simply because my father had? At sixteen, I could have called her. I could have written letters. I could have stood up to my father.

Why had I never stood up for what I wanted?

The dog was at my heels, her eyes fixed on me.

"Don't mind Bella," Jack said. "She's just trying to herd us."

"What?"

"It's what old swamp dogs do. Stop you from getting lost forever."

Her bobbed tail wagged.

I followed Jack as he climbed the stairs, distracted by the sway in his shoulders and his hips. He had an easy way about him, but he seemed as solid as the earth beneath us. His hands were solid too—those of a man who knew exactly what he was capable of, exactly how he could mold bare materials into what he wanted.

I loved feeling hands like those on my skin.

"There's a good bit to be done here, I guess," he said, pausing in the upstairs hallway. "I helped her with small things, like the cabinets and floors, but I didn't get into any big projects."

The banister was cool under my fingers. It was as big around as my thigh, carved in a Victorian style with simple lines. The spindles were square, not those dainty round ones that most people went for.

"I could probably be done in a couple of weeks," I said, peeking into the first upstairs bedroom. The bed was made up with a patchwork quilt, an antique desk and chair by the window. The curtains rippled like water in the breeze. It looked like it had been empty for years.

He laughed, shaking his head. "A couple of weeks? You won't find people around here who'll work that fast."

"No people. Just me."

He stopped cold. "You're going to fix all of this by yourself?"

"Sure." I wandered through the next room, a makeshift study and library. When I turned back to him, he was slack-jawed.

"What, you've never seen a woman fix a house?" I get a kick out of watching people's reactions when I tell them what I do. It was like the idea of a woman wielding a hammer and paintbrush for purposes that didn't include hanging pictures or painting with watercolor was too much to fathom. "I do this for a living," I said.

His mouth curled into a crooked smile that must have broken half the hearts in the parish. "Guess they don't make many like you any more, either," he said.

"I was sort of a tomboy growing up."

"Could have fooled me." His eyes drifted down to my feet, then back up to meet mine.

That look made me more aware of how my clothes stuck to me in this relentless heat. Not expecting to meet a soul today, I'd thrown on a thin camp-style shirt and an old pair of jeans with holes in the knees. Clothes were one of those details Dad claimed I overlooked. I rolled the sleeves up higher and placed my hands on my hips, staring him down.

"I wouldn't have taken you for the manual labor type," he said.

"I still like to get dirty. Some things never change."

He smiled and motioned for me to follow him down the hall. I noted the cracks in the plaster, the ancient light fixtures with their painted glass, the way Jack's broad shoulders strained the seams of his shirt.

His playfulness was disarming. He was so good-natured, even when he was about to be evicted. It felt easy to be with him, and for me that was rare.

"I think I have the answer," he said, leading me toward the back bedrooms. "It's win-win. You'll like it."

"Go on." One of the remaining bedrooms had a bed and dresser, an antique highboy with ball-and-claw feet. The last room was empty of furniture but full of boxes.

"How about I stay here while you do whatever work you need to do, and then you can turn me out into the cold, gator-infested bayou. While I'm here, I'll help you with the repairs. I'm pretty good with hammers and miter saws and whatnot."

"What makes you think I need any more hands?" Especially those hands, which I too easily envisioned gripping my hips instead of a hammer.

He led me back down the stairs. "Simple math. If, instead of you doing all this by yourself, you have me, then the work gets done twice as fast."

"Assuming you can take orders. And assuming your work is top-notch."

"Well, of course. And I figure you're going to need somebody who knows all the locals—what if you need a plumber or an electrician? You need a sub-contractor who can tell you who's reliable and who's gonna rip you off."

"Good point, but there's still one problem. I was going to stay here while I worked."

He raised an eyebrow.

"I can't stay here if you're here. And hotels will cost a fortune. That's not in the budget."

He nodded toward the upstairs. "You can stay here. It's not like we're short on rooms."

I laughed. "Stay here with you? Not a chance."

"What? I won't bite you, chère." He walked back onto the porch, pulled a cigarette from his pocket and lit it with a match. "Miss Vergie trusted me. You can trust me too."

"Bless her heart, but Grandma Vergie was a little bit nuts," I said.

She used to take in strays too—hell, that's probably where I got my inclination. She was one of those kind souls who never locked her doors and always trusted everybody to do right. I was slower to trust people and let them get close. I'd learned over and over that when you let people get close, they hurt you. They leave you. Friends said I was guarded, but to me that was just watching out for yourself. It made life less painful.

He shook the match, and the scent of sulfur and cloves filled the air between us. "I'll make you a deal," he said, holding his hand up in a Boy Scout salute. "If I misbehave, you can banish me to the couch at the firehouse. That's incentive enough to be good, believe me."

"The firehouse?"

He nodded. "Engine Six. On the other side of the canal."

"I wouldn't have taken you for a firefighter."

He stroked his chin. "Why, because of my squeaky-clean exterior?"

I tried to picture him in a fire truck. He seemed too laid back to squeeze himself into a state-regulated uniform.

"Can't a guy look a little rough around the edges on his day off?"

When I didn't reply, he said, "I get it. You think I'm just another hooligan trying to pull a fast one. You want to see my shield?"

"Actually, I do."

He pulled his wallet from his back pocket and flipped it open. A flash of brass caught my eye.

"Still, I don't even know you," I said, leaning against the porch rail. "I'm not in the habit of moving in with strange men."

"Well, I'm not accustomed to taking in strange women," he said. "But I'm willing to concede in order to help both of us out of a sticky situation. This way, you get to do your job, and I keep a roof over my head."

"Can't you stay at the firehouse for a few weeks?"

His eyebrows rose as he took a long drag on the cigarette. "It's kind of crowded right now," he said. "Got a few guys in the dog house and such. Happens about this time every year."

"In June?"

"I don't understand it, either."

"You have a copy of the lease?" I asked.

"Sure," he said. "It's around here somewhere."

"I'd like to see it."

He nodded, crushing the cigarette into the step. In the kitchen, he rooted through a drawer by the stove.

"I can't do this if I don't know anything about you," I said.

"OK," he said, thumbing through the papers. "Fair enough."

"I have questions."

He smiled. "I have answers."

I poured myself another glass of water. He stepped away from the drawer just long enough to pull a chair out from the table for me, like it was a reflex. The gesture struck me as tender, and then I realized why he seemed familiar.

"You were at the funeral," I said. Even though I'd banished the details from my mind, at unexpected moments, they would come pouring back.

He glanced up from the stack of papers and fixed his dark blue eyes on me. I remembered those eyes.

"You gave your seat to two little old ladies," I said.

He cocked his head and smiled. "You're the one that ran out in the storm. I was talking to your friend before she went after you."

I cringed at the memory. I'd been overwhelmed thinking about my mom leaving, Vergie dying and the possibility of running into my mother there. I'd dashed out of the church into a thunderstorm and stood on the lawn in the pouring rain until my friend Kate came out and dragged me to the car.

"You cut your hair," I said. "I didn't recognize you."

He shrugged. "It's OK. I didn't recognize you dry."

"I can't believe it's you," I said.

"I believe you had some questions for me."

It was easy to see why Vergie liked him. He was one of those guys who made you want to bake him a cake, who made you smile at bad pick-up lines. Some people just have a way about them that makes the world seem a little brighter. Vergie had also been one of those people.

"So you've been working for Vergie since you were seventeen?" I asked.

"Off and on." As he leaned against the table, it squeaked under his weight. "Started out doing odd jobs, then did more repairs when I got older. I'd come by and check on her a couple times a week and do whatever she needed done."

I watched his eyes to determine if he was lying. I was a good judge of character, but I'd been wrong once or twice, and it had made me gun shy, particularly when it came to smooth-talking, good-looking men.

"How long have you worked for the fire department?"

"Six years."

"Why did you come check on Vergie every week?"

"She looked out for me," he said. "So I looked out for her. It's what we do around here." He handed me the lease. "Here you go."

I turned to the back page and found Vergie's signature. Indeed, he had paid in advance. I searched for a clause that would void the lease upon the landlord's death, but there was none.

If what Jack said was true, how had I never seen him at the house all the summers I'd visited? He couldn't have been more than a couple of years older than me, and I would have remembered a teenage guy hanging around the house—especially when I was so boy-crazy I could hardly see straight.

According to the lease, he'd been renting six months. "What do you do besides fight fires?" I asked.

His fingers traced the stubble on his neck, until they disappeared in the collar of his shirt. When he spoke, he stared right at me, as if he was reading me just as carefully. "For work or play?"

I wondered if those terrible lines worked on women down here, or if they were reserved for out-of-towners who could be lulled into anything with a wink and a drawl.

"Either," I said.

"Nothing that's too embarrassing or impressive, chère." He half-smiled and opened the kitchen door, leading me back to the porch. We sat down on the steps. "But listen," he said, pulling a cigarette out, "you'll be safe here with me. And believe me, if you weren't, everybody in the parish would know about it, because everybody knows everybody's business out here on the bayou."

"Think I could bum one of those?" I nodded toward his cigarette.

"You're in luck... My last pack and then I quit."

He tapped another out, then leaned close as he cupped his hands around the match and lit the clove. I glanced up and caught his eyes for a moment through the smoke.

Clearly this had the potential for disaster—the kind that had nothing to do with the house. "Thanks," I said. "You were making me want one."

"So do I pass?"

I liked his quiet confidence. His eyes had a sleepy look about them, but there was a sharpness behind them as well—something that said I shouldn't mistake his easygoing manner for ignorance.

"Did you spend much time with her?" I asked him.

He smiled. "When she started renting to me, she came by to see me every Sunday. She said she was checking on the house, but I knew she was checking up on me. Your grandmother made a mean chicken pot pie."

"You knew her better than I did in the end." I wondered what they talked about, what he knew about her. If I let him stick around, I'd find out. That thought finally swayed me.

"I don't have much family of my own," he said. "She adopted me, you might say."

I could have been the one hearing all of Vergie's stories, instead of Jack Mayronne. If only I hadn't been so scared of my father.

"Come on, Enza," he said. "People here have boarders all the time. You're just renting me a room like anybody else would do if they had a big old house like this to themselves."

I took a long drag on the cigarette, watching the line of smoke rise toward the white porch ceiling. If Vergie trusted him to help her around the house, then he must be a decent man. She was always looking for the good in people, but she could spot the bad as quick as she spotted potato beetles in her garden.

I made a silent plea, hoping that wherever Vergie was, she could reach out and intervene if I was about to do something stupid. I waited for an instant, just in case a pipe burst or a vase went flying off the mantle as a kind of thump on the skull from the great hereafter. But there was nothing.

"Here's the deal, Mr. Mayronne. You help me with repairs,

and I'll give you six weeks to move out. If we finish before then, I'll refund your rent for the remaining days."

"What if it takes longer?"

"It won't."

"I could help you if it does," he said. "I owe a lot to Vergie. I'm not saying I can work for free, but I'll do you a better deal than anybody else around here."

"Six weeks is all I need," I said. "But if you like, we'll leave that option on the table."

"Fair enough," he said, extending his hand.

When we shook, his fingers tightened around mine, and a ripple passed through my arms and chest, like when a pebble is dropped in a pond.

He smiled. "This'll all work out fine. You'll see."

I almost believed him.

~

Chapter 3

After hauling my tool box and suitcases into the foyer, I paused at the bottom of the stairs to give the banister a shake. It was sturdy as a water oak. That was the thing about these old swamp houses: The plaster was cracking, and the walls weren't straight any more, but the woodwork was solid. The floors were made of heart pine boards eight inches wide. The ten-foot ceilings downstairs had carved crown molding that made my heart flutter. The upstairs bath had a clawfoot tub and a stained glass window that I wanted to cut out and take home with me. If those details had registered with me as a teenager, they'd been lost in the ether of young adulthood. In my memory, this had been a quaint little farm-style house—cute, but nothing special. Now, seeing its pocket doors and hand-carved moldings, I was smitten.

Stop, I told myself. *This has to be just another flip.*

Jack walked in behind me and grabbed my suitcases. "Let me give you a hand with that."

I followed him up to Vergie's old bedroom. Of the rooms upstairs, this one was the most furnished. It had the dresser, the highboy and the four-poster bed. Framed pictures hung over a vanity by the closet door, and books were stacked on the shelf of the nightstand.

Jack set the suitcases by the dresser and then opened two windows to get a cross-breeze. "Sorry it's so stuffy in here," he said. "I'll put the extra window unit in here so you won't melt."

"When I was a girl, I used to sneak in here to play," I told him. "I don't know why it seemed so magical at the time, but it was like Alice's rabbit hole."

Back then, I'd rummage through the closet and pick through the dresser drawers, but Vergie didn't mind. Her room had been a shrine to her travels, the shelves filled with trinkets from places I'd never heard of. Now, as I studied the dark wood and faded wallpaper, it looked like any old bedroom. The mystery had slipped away.

"I left everything in this room alone," Jack said.

"How come?"

"She told me to box everything up in here when I moved in, but I couldn't bring myself to do it." He leaned against the post of the canopy bed, ran his fingers along the carved vines. "I didn't need the space."

A collection of pictures sat by the lamp on the nightstand: a couple of me, and two black and white photos of my mother that I hadn't seen before. To me, my mother was a ghost. It was as if she'd vanished—*poof!*—like a dove under a magician's handkerchief. Dad refused to talk about her—ever.

I didn't forget about her, because how can you, really? But I tried.

After she left, Dad found ways to keep me busy in the summer so I wouldn't have time to think of those summers with Vergie. Jobs, college prep courses, internships. He scared me into thinking I needed all of those things to even dream of success, so I did what he told me. He said I was too old to do nothing in the summer, that if I didn't start working toward a goal, I'd end up as lost as my mother.

He used my mother as a threat.

Now, standing in this room that both was and was not Vergie's, it made me wonder: Had Vergie ever tried to see me, or had she quietly given in to my father's wishes? He could be cruel. He could sniff out people's weaknesses and drive them away, and he could have easily done that to Vergie.

I felt the pang that comes when you know you've done something terrible, and there's no real way to fix it.

I traced my fingers over a patchwork quilt that Vergie had almost certainly made. It was mostly blue and green, the log cabin pattern. The floorboards creaked when I walked across the room to the closet, where a half a dozen dresses still clung to wire hangers.

"This seemed bigger when I was a kid," I said.

"Things always do." Jack opened the drawer of the nightstand and handed me a key. His fingers brushed over my palm as he placed it there. "In case you want to lock yourself in."

"Thanks." I slipped the key into my pocket.

"I've got some leftovers downstairs," he said. "Nothing fancy, but it's better than going into town after driving all day."

"You're cooking me dinner?"

He smirked, heading back to the stairs. "I'm reheating your dinner. I'd take you to one of the local haunts, but I don't think you're ready for that crowd yet."

"Just as well," I said. "The last thing I want to do right now is get in a car." I followed him down the stairs, watching as the light caught flecks of red in his hair.

In the kitchen, Jack pulled a chair out from the table and motioned for me to sit. The floors were scuffed from these same spindle-backed chairs being dragged out from the table over the years. It was a small kitchen, but it had a walk-in pantry with floor-to-ceiling built-in cabinets. You just didn't see that any more.

Jack leaned over, rooting through the refrigerator. The clatter of pots caught my attention, but what held it was the way his jeans strained ever so slightly on his frame.

He put the pot on the stove and caught me staring.

I quickly looked away, my cheeks burning.

"Hope you like chili," he said. "I cook pretty simple."

"I won't complain when a guy's cooking dinner."

He stirred the chili and pulled two beers from the refrigerator. "Care for a drink?"

"After that drive today? You bet."

He hooked the caps together, popping both off at the same time like bartenders do when they're trying to impress. He passed me the beer, clinked his against it and said, "Here's to homecomings."

His knee brushed mine as he sat down across from me. His eyes looked as blue-green as the bottles, and I found myself staring too long again.

"I know this must be little strange for you," he said.

"It wasn't what I was expecting."

"Few things around here are."

The white cabinets were chipped and stained, but the appliances were still in good shape. The sink was original—a huge one that extended into countertops, with grooves to channel the water from drying dishes back into the basin. The old pie safe was still in the corner, where Vergie used to keep her pies, and later her cookbooks. Patterns of stars and triangles were punched in the tin panels.

"I miss this place," I said. "Didn't realize how much until today."

"When's the last time you were here?"

"I was sixteen. I can't believe it's been fifteen years." The dog, Bella, wandered back into the room and sat down at my feet. She stared at me, as if still deciding whether I was a threat. "I should have come back to visit more. I should have ignored my father."

He cocked his head.

"Long story," I said, waving my hand between us. "He forbade me to come back here, and I was too young and stupid to rebel."

"It's hard to see what's really important when you're that age. Sometimes you still can't see it when you've grown up."

"Is this where you tell me your family's just as messed up as mine?"

"My parents died a long time ago."

"Shit. I'm sorry. I only meant—"

"It's OK," he said, getting up to stir the chili. "It just taught me you have to get your priorities in order. Be honest in your relationships."

"Did you grow up around here?"

"Yeah." He sounded relieved to change the subject. "Down in Terrebonne. Moved up here and went to high school, then left for college. I bounced around a little but came back here to work at the fire department a few years ago." He filled two bowls with chili and brought them to the table.

"I thought firemen lived in a firehouse."

"Only when I'm on duty. One day on and two days off."

"I'm lucky I came here on your day off. You would have given me a heart attack if you'd showed up in the middle of the night."

"You and me both." He grinned. "You gonna start this work tomorrow, you say?"

I took a long drink of the beer. Lately I could never turn off my working self—too much of my father had rubbed off on me. I thought about lumber prices when I sat down to dinner, estimated shipping costs when I lay down to sleep.

"First thing," I said.

"You don't waste any time, huh?"

"Not with houses. All those people that told us time is money—they were right." Already I was calculating how much paint it would take to cover the kitchen, how long it would take to refinish the hall floors. The old wallpaper needed to be stripped, and all the rooms needed a fresh coat of paint. People loved these houses with hand-carved woodwork because it made them feel like they owned a piece of dying history, but they expected a combination of historical and practical. They wanted hot tubs, updated kitchens and walk-in closets. I wasn't planning to knock out walls, but this house needed a visual overhaul that would preserve the best parts of the architecture while bringing it into this century.

"How's the chili?" he asked.

"Spicy."

"Need a glass of milk?"

I laughed. "I haven't been away that long."

He grinned, finishing his beer. "Tomorrow we'll go to the hardware store across the canal. I know the owner."

I had a credit card with one of the regional chain stores but kept quiet. He was making a nice gesture.

"Great," I said. "I'm on a tight budget."

After that, a silence settled between us, like we were two teenagers on a blind date, neither knowing what to say. I tried not to stare at Jack, but it took all of my willpower to avoid his eyes. A friend once told me I was intimidating because I stared too long. *It's no wonder you don't have a boyfriend,* she said, *You stare men down.* Ever since then I'd made myself look away every so often.

So I forced myself to break his gaze. He smiled once when he caught me looking at his hands, as if he knew I was imagining what they would feel like against my skin.

I shook the thought away. I'd avoided getting too close to men for a long time, keeping them at a distance even as I let them live in my house. My penchant for distance came from my father. After my mother left us, he'd blamed it on her being heartless. He'd convinced me that if you let people get close to your heart, they'd hurt you. I was tired of being hurt, so I chose relationships that on some level I knew would only be short-term. They were predictable: I kept the guy close but not too close; I liked him, but I was detached. When we inevitably split, I was lonely but not heartbroken.

The pattern I'd learned was this: When you let people get close, they love you, then they hurt you, then they leave you. When they disappear, they take a part of you with them, and you can never get it back. It had happened with my mother. It had happened with friends. Boyfriends. Vergie.

If I'd spent more time with Vergie, I might be more trusting. Less cold. My father resented her because of my mother. I could see it in the way he bristled when I mentioned coming here that last time when I was sixteen. *Your mother turned her whole family against us,* he'd said to me. *Those bridges are burned.*

And because he was the one who didn't leave, I trusted him.

"Hey, Enza, you all right?" Jack Mayronne was staring at me like he thought I might break at any second.

"Sorry," I said. "I'm not good company tonight." Those thoughts had been pushed so far down for so long that now it felt like they were tearing through my skin to get out.

"It's OK. I won't take it personally." His smile was warm as he stood and gathered up our dirty dishes.

"I'm just tired. I think I'll turn in for the night."

He placed the dishes in the sink and said, "So I'll see you bright and early?"

"Crack of dawn." I pushed my chair under the table and took the half-empty beer with me.

"Good night, chère. Sleep tight."

The dog whined, sitting on her haunches.

"Bella will protect you," he said. "It's one of her favorite things to do."

"Good night, Jack." I trudged up the stairs, hoping this wasn't another huge mistake. The sound of his name on my lips had sent a shiver along my skin. *Get a hold of yourself.*

The clatter of toenails on heart pine rang in my ears as the dog bounded up the stairs behind me. She paused at Vergie's door.

"Planning to spy on me?"

Her ears pricked forward.

"Git," I said, turning the doorknob.

She snorted and slinked back down the stairs.

I peeled off my sticky clothes and tossed them onto the rocking chair. On the wall above it was a grouping of framed photos. In one black and white picture, a five-year-old version of me was riding a billy goat, one hand grasping the fur on its neck, one hand up in the air like a bull rider. Barefoot, my hair in pigtails. Closing my eyes, I could feel the coarse fur in my fingers. Harold the goat had served as a pony back then, bucking as I rode him around the yard. By the end of summer, I'd been covered in scratches from the blackberry bushes where he threw me. Even now, standing in the musty bedroom, I could feel the wind tickle my ears, hear the goat's hooves pounding the dirt beneath them.

I made up the bed with the sheets Jack had left stacked on the dresser and opened the window higher. I locked the door and laid the key on the nightstand. The cool sheets soothed me as I climbed into bed. I didn't expect Jack to creep upstairs in the middle of the night, but still I listened for footsteps on the stairs. He seemed like one of the good guys, but how could I be sure? What if he had another key? I flipped off the bedside lamp and tried not to think any more about Jack, thinking instead of those long forgotten summers. With my eyes closed, I felt the salty breeze warm against my skin, heard the pounding of goat hooves in a thicket, growing closer, as if to carry me off into a distant memory.

∾

Read more about Enza and Jack in
Bayou My Love: A Bayou Sabine Novel:
bit.ly/bayoumylove

Acknowledgments

Thanks always to my family and friends, who are the most loving and supportive people I know. A special thank you to my friend and fellow author Katie Rose Guest Pryal, who is my best first reader. Thank you to Andrew, who always provides a lantern for the writerly path, even when I have doubts and dark days.

Thanks to Velvet Morning Press, for publishing the first edition of this book.

And, as always, thank you to my readers, who inspire me to keep doing what I love, and to keep telling the stories that are so much fun to tell.

About the Author

Lauren divides her time between writing, teaching, and printmaking. She is the author of the Bayou Sabine Series, which includes the novels *Bayou My Love* and *Bayou Whispers*.

Originally from South Carolina, she has worked as an archaeologist, an English teacher, and a ranger for the National Park Service. She earned her MFA in creative writing from Georgia College & State University, and her MFA in Book Arts from The University of Alabama.

She won the *Family Circle* short fiction contest, was a finalist for the Novello Festival Press First Novel Award, and was nominated for an AWP Intro Award. She's a sucker for a good love story and is happiest when she writes comedy and romance. She lives in North Carolina, where she's at work on the next novel in the Bayou Sabine series.

~

sign up for Lauren's author newsletter,
Writing Down South:
tinyletter.com/firebrandpress

~

Books by Lauren Faulkenberry

- BAYOU MY LOVE: A Bayou Sabine Novel
- BACK TO BAYOU SABINE: A Bayou Sabine Novella
- BAYOU, WHISPERS FROM THE PAST: A Bayou Sabine Novel
- JUST THE TROUBLE I NEEDED: A Bayou Sabine Novella
- BENEATH OUR SKIN and Other Stories

www.laurenfaulkenberry.com